A SPRINKLING OF COALDUST

Wendy John

Amazon

Copyright © 2023 Wendy John

All rights reserved

The characters and events portrayed in this book are fictitious. Any similarity to real persons, living or dead, is coincidental and not intended by the author.

No part of this book may be reproduced, or stored in a retrieval system, or transmitted in any form or by any means, electronic, mechanical, photocopying, recording, or otherwise, without express written permission of the publisher.

ISBN-13: 9798391782155
ISBN-10: 1477123456

Cover design by: Art Painter
Library of Congress Control Number: 2018675309
Printed in the United States of America

*I would like to dedicate this book
to Colin for his continued patience
during the writing of this book.*

CHAPTER ONE

Condensation ran down the windowpane as steam permeated the room as the pot bubbled away on the black leaded fireplace in the small room of the miner's cottage. Megan wiped the perspiration from her brow with her slender fingertips. Tendrils of hair which had fallen loose from the bun at the nape of her neck, formed ringlets around her pretty face. With her deep brown eyes and olive complexion you would have thought she was of Mediterranean origin instead of pure Welsh blood.

Megan took the last saucepan full of boiling water from the hearth and tipped it carefully into the old tin bath just in time for the arrival of her husband Evan, and her father-in-law as they entered the front door.

Both weary after working an arduous twelve-hour shift down the mine. Evan and William were covered from head to foot in coaldust, their features barely distinguishable from the coaldust etched into their faces. Her father-in-law removed his jacket and cap and placed them onto the hearth. It was a daily ritual in the Roberts' household to take it in turns to use the bath water first and tonight it was Evans's turn. Her father-in-law took his clay pipe from the mantelpiece and walked slowly into the garden to sit on the bench, to savour the sweet breath of fresh clean air.

As Megan looked into Evan's face, she saw a twinkle in his deep blue eyes, and he gave her a smile that melted her heart. He placed his hand inside his pocket, then held Megan's hand and placed something into her palm, he then closed her fingers tightly around it. Megan could feel the cold metal but could scarcely believe it. She could feel the excitement bubbling up inside her, as she realised what it was. Anyone would think Megan had been given the keys to the kingdom of heaven, instead of the key to the front door of their new home. Evan told Megan to calm down, he knew she would be excited at the prospect of them finally having a new home of their own and he did not want her to get her hopes up. Evan went on to explain that they would not be moving to one of the new cottages that had recently been built up on the ridge. Instead, they had been given the key to Number 3, Mill Row. These were older cottages that were once owned by William Malin during his time as owner of the old ironworks. Since the ironworks had closed, they had now been requisitioned by the Coal Board and were rented out to the families of the collieries in the area.

As Megan digested the news, she initially felt disappointed, as she had her heart set on one of the new cottages. Then the realisation set in that herself Evan and the children would be having their own home at long last. She felt the urge to jump up and down grab hold of Evan and dance around the room, but she curtailed herself as she looked into the ever-watchful eye of her mother-in-law.

Since the day they had married she had resided with her mother-in-law Margaret, and for this she would be eternally grateful. Housing in 1880's Wales was scarce this was due to two factors. One was before this time there had been extraordinarily little industry in the South Wales Valleys.

Then copper and iron ore were discovered and the whole landscape changed. Where there was once small farmhouses and green fields, now mine shafts had been sunk. Copper and Ironworks built taking over the countryside. Nobody complained this was the dawn of a new era. It might have looked ugly, unhealthy, and sometimes dark and gloomy due to the pollution in the air, but for the people of Wales this heralded a time of change. There was plenty of work for all the men, they were earning a good wage and for the first time were able to provide for their families. It might have seemed idyllic scraping a living off the land, but times had been hard, and children often went hungry.

The other factor that contributed to the housing shortage was the influx of families from other areas. People had moved from the West Country to the prosperity of Wales, and whole communities of Irish wanting to escape the poverty of the potato famine had come to Wales looking for a better life.

Megan looked towards Evan then kissed his cheek and smiled as she walked towards the mantelpiece clutching her precious key and placed it there. She did not know what to say to Margaret who was standing there watching her, holding Dafydd's hand and carrying nine-month-old Bronwen in her arms. Megan simply smiled at her and gently kissed her cheek.

Margaret was a difficult woman to love even though Megan had lived with her for the past five years, she felt no closer to her now than when she first moved in. Margaret was a plain woman with sharp bird like features. Tall and thin she always walked with her back as straight as a ramrod. Many a time she had rebuked Megan telling her to hold her shoulders back and walk straight. Margaret had a sour disposition and never became excited or emotional over anything. Megan had tried to change Margaret during the first two years that she had lived with her but realised that this was Margaret's nature and no matter how hard she tried she was never going to succeed in changing her personality.

Evan had two elder brothers Bryn and Owen. Bryn was tall with the same stance and features as his mother. He was arrogant, abrupt and could be quite rude at times. Megan had never liked Bryn and was amazed how he had married Elizabeth who was such a sweet natured person, this was beyond Megan's comprehension. His other brother Owen was the complete opposite, he was also tall with jet black hair and chestnut brown eyes, he most certainly had not inherited his mother's looks. A handsome man would be the words Megan would use to describe Owen. In fact, him and Evan were so alike they could have been twins. Except that Evan was slightly shorter than Owen and of a stockier build like his father.

Both Owen and Evan were like their father in many ways. Being quiet and gently spoken and slow to lose their tempers. Both were also very mischievous in their ways. It was this quality that had first attracted Megan to Evan when she had first laid eyes upon him. Also, he had inherited his father's sapphire blue eyes.

Whereas Megan had always found it difficult to love Margaret it was the complete opposite with her father-in-law William. He was a kind gentle man who never raised his voice. Megan could never understand how he did not stand up to Margaret who could be nasty and sharp tongued at times. William would look straight into Margaret's eyes, take the telling off then just nod his head and walk away. This made Margaret even angrier, and it always amused Megan.

Megan often wondered if the reason Margaret was so miserable was when Evan was ten years old, she had given birth to twin daughters. It had been a difficult birth Margaret had nearly died during childbirth. Sadly, the girls were tiny frail babies and only lived a couple of hours. Megan could understand why Margaret was so bitter and being fortunate to have a baby daughter of her own, she knew there must have been times over the years when Margaret thought what might have been if her girls had lived. Even though she idolised her three sons there must have been a sad longing in her heart for her daughters.

CHAPTER TWO

During the latter part of the Nineteenth Century the once small hamlet of Cefn Cribbwr in South Wales had grown considerably. Several small groups of houses had now been built by the rich landowners, who had seized the opportunity for development due to Cefn's influx of visitors.

Evan's parents occupied a small cottage at the bottom of a steep hill known as Bedford Road. Fortunately, Megan and Evan's new cottage was only a short walk away from his parent's house which Megan was pleased about because Margaret with all her faults was always on hand to help look after the children.

Margaret looked at Megan and could see how excited she was and told her as soon as they had all eaten, she would take care of the children for Megan and Evan to go and see their new home. Megan was so happy, but once again resisted the urge to give Margaret a hug and simply smiled and thanked her instead.

It was a beautiful September evening as Megan and Evan walked hand in hand down the lane towards their new home. Mill Row consisted of just six cottages; this was minor compared to the mining areas in the Rhondda Valley. Some of the rows of houses there contained more than fifty cottages. Megan and Evan watched as two small boys walked past them proudly holding a bucket that they had just filled from the well. Another group of children ran past them engrossed in their game of tag. Whilst another larger group of children sat on the grass verge heads bent closely together shouting and arguing over a game of marbles. A young woman stood outside one of the cottages gently rocking a fractious baby in her arms, she simply nodded to them and continued with her task desperately trying to comfort the small infant.

Megan's hand was shaking in anticipation as she turned the key in the lock. As the door slowly creaked open, she gasped as she looked inside. This was certainly not what she had imagined. The floor was covered in dust. The range was encased with caked on food and grease. The previous owners had not even bothered to rake out the embers from the fire. It was also very dark inside the small cottage, but Megan could see why. The windows were so dirty and dusty that no sunlight was able to shine through them. They walked through to the scullery; the large sink also looked like it had never been cleaned. Apart from the dirty windows and dusty floorboards the two bedrooms upstairs were habitable. Megan could see the concerned look on Evan's face, she knew he had hoped it would have been more presentable.

She told Evan with a lot of challenging work she would have a perfect home for them all in a couple of days.

When they got back to Margaret's home Megan explained about the state of their new home. Margaret told her she would take care of the children for the next couple of days to enable Megan to get their cottage cleaned in readiness for them to move in.

Over the next couple of weeks Megan worked tirelessly, scrubbing the flagstones until the floors sparkled. She cleaned and black leaded the range until it looked like new. Now the windows were free from dirt and dust the sunlight shone through the small panes of glass.

On his day off Evan had lit a fire in the grate and the warmth and glow from the fire gave the small room a comforting homely feel. Evan and Owen had brought in the furniture both laughing and joking as Megan gave instructions as to where each item was to be placed. It had certainly been a busy two weeks. Now at long last Megan had the perfect home she had waited so patiently for. All she required was some pretty curtains and her cottage would be complete.

It was a beautiful sunny day and Megan strolled towards Bedford Road calling in to see Margaret on her way. She gave her a hug and thanked her for taking care of the children which enabled Megan to get the cottage habitable. Margaret told Megan she would look after the children to enable her to purchase the curtain material, then her new home would then be complete. With a smile on her face and a spring in her step Megan walked to Mr Thomas who owned the small Drapers' shop in Cefn Road.

The doorbell tinkled as she walked into the small shop. Megan loved the aroma of the variety of materials stored inside the shop. Her eyes surveyed all the neatly stacked shelves holding an array of fabrics consisting of heavy-duty materials for work clothes. Serviceable hardwearing cloths for ladies' dresses. Then there was material for special occasions such as weddings and church going and Easter time. Mr Thomas usually had quite a dour expression but Megan's cheery disposition when she entered the shop seemed to rub off on him and nothing was too much trouble when it came to serving Megan. Megan glanced up at the top shelf and a brightly coloured material with yellow flowers on it caught her eye. She imagined how spectacular it would look in the bedrooms. It was obviously a rarely bought fabric as Mr Thomas had to brush the dust off it when he brought it down from the top shelf. He told Megan as it was not a popular range Megan could buy it for half the price. She was so excited she purchased extra and went overboard with the material.

Megan spent every evening meticulously sewing together the material she had purchased from Mr Thomas. Megan had thought that the material was so pretty she got a little carried away once she had completed the bedroom curtains, she decided to make curtains for the little living room as well. The transformation of their new home was now complete. When Megan took Evan to see what she had achieved with all her hard work. He was amazed at the difference, as they opened wide their front door sunlight shone through the small window panes and the yellow flowers of the brightly coloured curtains gave the room an added touch of decadence. Megan had also made cushions to match from the left-over material and they were placed neatly onto the settle underneath the front window. As Megan turned to look at Evans smiling face, she knew all her arduous work had been worthwhile. Dafydd started running around in circles excited to be in an unfamiliar environment and Bronnie started crawling along the floor towards the wooden settle and pulled herself up. It certainly would not be long until she would be taking her first steps.

There was a knock on the front door, and they were greeted by the robust figure of Mrs Davies from next door holding a large black saucepan in her hand. Her words to them were "don't worry my lovelies I am not coming in to visit this is just some lamb cawl I have made for your tea tonight to save you cooking". Megan thanked her and gave her a hug then Mrs Davies wobbled away as she headed back inside her home next door. Megan then turned to Evan and told him she was going to be incredibly happy in her new home. Thankfully both the children were sleeping peacefully by 8:00 o'clock that evening. The air outside was warm which enabled Megan and Evan to sit outside in the small garden behind the house. Fortunately, it was a calm night and there was no wind so the smell from the communal toilets was not lingering in the air.

They both crept up the steep wooden staircase being careful not to disturb the children. Megan took in the scene around her. Even though it was only a small bedroom the pretty quilt that Margaret had made for them adorned the bed. Megan walked towards the small window and closed the curtains. They made love like a couple of newlyweds it was such a long-awaited pleasure as Megan could never relax with the children in their room and knowing that Evan's parents were in the room next door. They fell asleep contentedly wrapped in each other's arms.

Evan kissed Megan gently on the cheek at 5:00 AM the next morning as he sent off to go to the Colliery. Megan drifted back off to sleep until she was woken by Bronnie crying to be fed. As Dafydd was still sleeping she picked Bronnie up and crept back into her bedroom where Bronnie snuggled contentedly into her breast.

Margaret had told Megan she would be visiting today so Megan rushed around making sure the cottage was spick and span for Margaret's inspection.

Margaret's face was a picture, Megan's choice of curtain material was far too bright for her liking but to be honest they did look very pretty on the small front window and the matching cushions brightened up the room. She could not believe it when she went upstairs, and the bright yellow flowered curtains adorned both bedroom windows. Megan was smiling obviously pleased with her choice of material Margaret being her usual self simply looked at Megan then shook her head in total disbelief.

After spending a couple of days in her new home Megan started to appreciate Margaret, only now she realised how much Margaret had helped with all the household chores alongside caring for the children she now found the children difficult Dafydd was running around inside and outside the house. On one occasion by the time, she had scooped Bronnie up from the floor and proceeded to run after Dafydd, she could hear angry shouts coming from one of the toilet doors as Dafydd stood outside banging on the door and laughing. This most certainly would not have occurred if Margaret had been around, she only had to raise her voice and Dafydd behaved. Megan shouted words of apology to the occupant of the toilet and dragged a screaming Dafydd back to the house. Mair Davies from next door had very kindly offered to look after the children for Megan to get on with her chores, but Megan had declined the offer. Poor Mair had no control whatsoever over her little brood she certainly had her hands full with three little ones and another one due in two month's time. Maybe it was because of her total laidback attitude with nothing phasing her that enabled Mair to cope with it all. She was the most amazing cook and lovely smells always wafted from her cottage; the little ones always appeared holding a large chunk of freshly baked bread in their grubby little hands. Mair also had it tough with her husband who was a complete waste of space. He was a hard worker the same as the other miners but every Friday once he had collected his wages, he would make his way to the White Lion public house on Bedford Road and would not leave until the landlord kicked him out at closing time. Gwilym's dulcet tones could be heard coming down the hill towards the cottages he would be singing at the top of his voice oblivious to the angry shouts of various neighbours on his way home. Then loud voices from both Mair and Gwilym could be heard as he entered the cottage. Then magically after about half an hour all would go quiet as Gwilym fell into bed in a drunken stupor. Megan felt so sorry for Mair, and appreciated the wonderful considerate husband she had in Evan.

Megan often wondered to herself what the neighbours on the other side thought of this behaviour. They were the complete opposite. Rachel and Thomas had only been married for two years and had not been blessed with a family yet. They were a very contented couple both had been brought up in a small village in West Wales. Thomas had moved here to work at Parc Slip mine although he was not your typical miner by any means. He was a quiet softly spoken man, and a lay preacher, he went around the different chapels every Sunday spreading the word. Evan unfortunately could not take to Thomas as he found his kind of religion to be overpowering. The trouble was you could not have a normal conversation with Thomas as he always wanted to try to convert you to his way of thinking. Both Megan and Evan had both been brought up in the Welsh Chapels and enjoyed their Chapel meetings every Sunday evening. Then meeting friends after the service for tea and cake, so it was not as if they were heathens. Rachel and Thomas seemed to have their own group of friends and they had regular meetings at their cottage twice a week. In all fairness both Rachel and Thomas always invited all the neighbours in Mill Row to join them. Unfortunately, most of them declined their offer, neither of them was put off by this and whenever you saw them a cordial welcome was always extended. Megan liked Rachel she found her to be a sweet natured person but sadly Rachel did not seem to have the courage to do what she wanted it seemed as if she was afraid to go against Thomas's wishes and very often when Thomas was at the mine Rachel would ask Megan in for a cup of tea and cake, she always made a great fuss over the children both Dafydd and Bronnie loved spending time with Rachel.

Megan had no chance to acquaint herself with the rest of the neighbours yet. The only ones she had heard of from Mair were Mr and Mrs Williams at the end of the street. Mr Williams was known by everyone in the village as Tommy pigs since he had been fortunate enough to live on the end house which had a piece of waste ground adjoining it, and to supplement his income had kept three pigs. Everyone complained in the summer due to the smell, but Tommy pigs was no fool and he kept his neighbours sweet by supplying them with offal from the pigs when he slaughtered one. His wife Alice was also known by the inhabitants of Mill Row as she paid visits to her neighbours inquiring if they had any vegetable peelings, she could have to help feed the pigs. Alice was an exceptionally beautiful woman with blonde hair and blue eyes and a very curvaceous figure, Tommy pigs was envied by most of the men in the small village of Cefn.

CHAPTER THREE

Although Megan had waited for her own home for so long, she hated being stuck in all day, so weather permitting she would take the children and walk across the fields to an area of open ground known locally as "The Waun". It was so quiet and peaceful there. Megan would take a small picnic for lunch then sit and listen to the birds while Dafydd and Bronnie who is now walking explored their surroundings. The only problem was Megan would spend so much time at the Waun she would lose all track of the time and found herself struggling to cook dinner and prepare Evan's bath. She was lucky that Evan was a patient man he never moaned or complained about the complete chaos that greeted him when he got home from the mine. He would help with the cooking and looked after the children whilst Megan organised the hot water for his bath. Megan promised Evan that she would try to be more organised.

Sunday arrived and the children were very well behaved at the service mainly because they were sitting alongside Margaret and William. After Chapel they all went back to Margaret's house for Sunday lunch. Looking around the neat cottage with all the ready prepared dinner organised Megan made a promise to herself that from tomorrow she would try to be a better housekeeper for Evan.

Bryn was his usual obnoxious self, taking over the conversation. The one thing that bothered Megan was Owen he was not his usual cheery self and seemed to be quite distracted and withdrawn. Megan discussed her concerns with Evan when she got back to their house. Evan told her he had also noticed that something was bothering Owen and he would pursue the matter further and try and find out what was wrong.

Even though the sun was shining Megan stayed indoors and cleaned the cottage, prepared food and had a bath ready for Evan. He teased her when he got home and said he must have entered the wrong cottage. He kissed her gently on the cheek and Megan hugged him. They had just settled the children down for the night and were enjoying sitting by the fireside reading when they heard a gentle tap on the front door.

Megan and Evan were both surprised and concerned to see Owen standing in the doorway. Megan preceded to make a cup of tea and placed a few slices of Bara Brith on a plate Owen sat down and said he needed to discuss something with them both, he apologised for his low mood over the past couple of weeks but explained he had a lot on his mind that he had needed to get sorted. He could see the worried expressions on both Evan and Megan's faces. So, he quickly went on to explain it was nothing serious, he had no health problems, nor were there any problems at the mine. It was more an affair of the heart. Whilst Evan still looked serious and concerned Megan simply smiled. Owen took Megan's hand and gave her one of his endearing smiles saying, "typical woman when it comes to any sort of romantic liaison." Megan and Evan listened intently whilst Owen explained his dilemma. Owen told them both for the past six months he had been courting Abigail Parry. Megan and Evan exchanged glances and could now understand Owen's dilemma. Abigail Parry was the daughter of Thomas Parry the owner of Brynddu Mine. All of them knew this was an impossible situation Abigail was way above Owen's status as a mine worker she was Gentry, and they knew her father would have plans in place for any future husband for her. Whether it was another mine owner or mine manager or a landowner with a country estate. It certainly would not be a labourer or mine worker Megan asked Owen if this was just a passing fancy or had he fallen in love with Abigail, and due to Owen's serious mood over the past few months Megan knew it was the latter. Owen told them both he knew the seriousness of the situation and both him and Abigail were aware of what problems would be in store should her father find out. Owen said they had broken off their courtship for several weeks, but this did not work as they had fallen in love with each other. He said they had talked about moving away to get married, but this would mean both leaving their families behind which would put a strain on their relationship. Owen said Abigail and he had discussed all options and decided to wait a few more months then Owen was going to approach Thomas Parry and ask for his daughter's hand in marriage. A frightening and dauntless task. Owen knew deep down that Thomas Parry would certainly not agree to this and he would be putting his livelihood on the line. Megan agreed with Owen she knew Thomas Parry had a reputation and was not liked in the village.

He was not an easy man to like, he was not one of those people who had worked their way up in this world. He had been fortunate enough to be a beneficiary of his uncle's will and had been left the house and the land on which the Brynddu Mine had been sunk. He was arrogant and full of self-importance, what he wanted he took no matter what the consequences. Megan felt so sorry for Owen he could have had his pick of any girl in the village why did he have to get involved with Abigail Parry and furthermore fall in love with her. This was a total disastrous situation and one that was doomed from day one. Megan put her arms around Owen and thanked him for confiding in them both. She asked him if his parents knew about this but even before Owen shook his head, she knew the answer was no. They both said that they would support him, and he was welcome to visit them with Abigail unseen by anyone in the village, but also begged him to take things slowly think carefully and think of both him and Abigail's future.

CHAPTER FOUR

Even though Megan felt content in her new home, things were starting to change around her and making her feel unsettled. Owen had now left Brynddu Mine and was working at Parc Slip Colliery in Aberkenfig. Both Megan and Evan knew his main reason for leaving Brynddu was to distance himself from anything to do with Thomas Parry. He had told the family that working conditions were better at Parc Slip, with shorter hours and more pay. His departure had unsettled Evan as Evan had worked alongside Owen since first going down the mine when they were only boys of fourteen. Megan felt a sense of uneasiness every time Evan came home from the mine. He was not his usual happy self. He was full of complaints saying he like did not like the new chap who was Owen's replacement.

Then a month after Owen had gone to Parc Slip, Evan came home from work in a brighter mood. Megan felt relieved and hoped he was now settling into working without Owen.

The children had been settled down for the night and the evenings were now drawing in. September and October were unusually mild months, but it was now the start of November and it had certainly arrived with a vengeance. The one main compensation of being a miner's wife was the concession they had on coal, always having plenty stockpiled in the small coal house in readiness for the chilly winter months ahead. Megan looked across at Evan his feet comfortably placed on the hearth to enjoy the heat from the fire. Evan's head was bent over reading his book. Megan seated herself opposite him. As she sat down Evan got up and walked towards the table and put his book down then slowly walked back towards Megan. Megan was slightly perturbed at the serious look on his face. He knelt in front of her and took her hands placing them in his. Evan said he had made a decision and hoped Megan would be happy with it. Evan told her they were looking for men to start in Parc Slip and he had been thinking about it for the last week. He went on to explain that he had spoken to Owen who told him working conditions were far better at Parc Slip than they were at Brynddu. Megan smiled at Evan she could tell this was something he really wanted to do. Nevertheless, she felt uneasy about this decision, mainly because she hated any sort of change. Although she knew Evan was right the pay was better and with less hours, they would be able to spend more time with the children.

That night Megan tossed and turned and was unable to sleep, she had only just drifted off to sleep when Evan kissed her on the cheek and left for work. Megan heard the sound of a hooter in the distance, this was the noise everybody dreaded the warning sound coming from the mine informing everyone then there had been an accident at the mine. Megan wrapped her shawl around her shoulders. Her feet felt like lead as she ascended Bedford Hill, she felt like she was running in slow motion. As she got to the top of the Hill the church door is open and bodies are being laid out. She looks down the Hill and sees more bodies arriving being pushed on handcarts. As she stands there staring in the distance, she hears children crying. It is getting louder and louder then she feels someone pulling on her arm. Megan looks down and sees Dafydd standing there holding Bronnie's hand they are both crying. To her relief Megan realises she has been dreaming her nightdress is soaked with perspiration and she is shaking. Relieved she scoops the children up into her arms and holds them close to comfort them. Megan was terribly upset when Dafydd told her she had frightened them because she had been shouting and crying in her sleep. It took some time for Megan to calm them both down. Megan had never had a nightmare like that before but comforted herself with the fact it was due to the discussion she had had with Evan last night regarding the changes he was going to make.

Megan tried to put all thoughts of last night's dream out of her mind, but she could not concentrate on anything. In the end she decided to go and visit Margaret. As she entered Margaret's spotless little cottage, the smell of freshly baked bread entered her nostrils. A large saucepan of broth was gently simmering on the stove. A strange feeling of home sickness entered Megan's body which seemed strange. As all she had ever wanted to do for the five years, she was living with Margaret was to escape to her own home. As she sat with a cup of tea in her hands and watched the children playing on the floor with a wooden truck that William had made, she felt very emotional.

Even though Margaret was such a difficult woman to live with everything had always been organised. Only now did Megan realise how lucky she had been. Her and Margaret had always shared the chores, taking it in turns to clean and black lead the kitchen range. Preparing the evening meal together and looking after the children. Megan started to cry she told Margaret about her nightmare in the early hours of this morning and how it had upset the children.

Megan was completely taken aback by the show of emotion this was not the Margaret she remembered. Maybe Margaret was missing Megan and the children. Margaret explained to Megan bad dreams and worries were not unusual for a miner's wife. Over the years she had spent many a sleepless night worrying about William and the boys working in the mines. Especially when there had been accidents or an explosion in any of the surrounding mines. Margaret went on to explain every miner's wife experienced the same worrying feeling in their stomachs when husbands left the house in the morning for a twelve-hour shift down the mines. Margaret said the most difficult period of her life had been when the boys reached fourteen and she had no choice but to send them to work in the mines. She said she would never forget seeing them descending the hill carrying their lamps in one hand and a bait box in the other. She said she could not bear to see them coming home from work. Their little legs barely able to manage the hill to the cottage. Coaldust etched into every pore of their tiny bodies. Margaret said it used to break her heart as she washed them every evening in the bath by the fireside. Margaret said she went to bed in the night and closed her eyes trying to picture another existence with her family living on a farm in the countryside inhaling fresh clean air everyday instead of coal dust.

Megan stayed and had lunch with Margaret. They enjoyed some of her delicious broth and freshly baked bread, the children tucked into their meal and seemed content and no worse for their upset earlier this morning. Margaret said there was enough bread and broth left over for Megan to take home for Evan. As she was leaving Megan hugged Margaret and thanked her for making her feel better. She walked down the hill feeling uplifted clutching the children's hands. She did not mention her dream to Evan that evening, she just told him she had spent a lovely day talking and enjoying lunch with his mother. Evan looked at Megan with a perplexed expression on his face it was most unusual for Megan to describe a visit to his mother's home in this way.

CHAPTER FIVE

Christmas was quickly approaching. Over the past couple of weeks Megan had felt more settled everything seemed to be going well for Evan and Owen in their new employment at Parc Slip and it would be nice to have extra money coming in to help with Christmas.

Megan had been busy making a doll for Bron and Evan and Owen had been helping William build a small car for Dafydd. Both Megan and Margaret had also been busy making Christmas puddings and cakes for all the family.

All the family had attended Chapel for the Christmas Carol service then went back to Margaret's home for tea. Owen was putting on a brave face, although it must have been difficult for him not being able to bring Abigail to the family get togethers. Megan had hope because of the tricky situation Owen's romance would have phased out but sadly this did not seem to be the case, in fact Owen told them he would be speaking to Thomas Parry in the new year and would be asking his permission to court Abigail. He said they were both so happy together and fed up with hiding their courtship from everyone. Bryn was a changed man, after being married for 11 years Elizabeth was now pregnant and looking forward to being a mother in the spring. Evan and Megan were both looking forward to their first Christmas in their new home.

As Megan got out of bed on Christmas morning a wave of sickness washed over her, she felt light headed and dizzy she hoped it would soon pass as she had so much to do. She wanted everything to be special in their new home. The children excitedly unwrapped their presents, Bron was too young to understand but as Dafydd started jumping around and shouting she joined in with him.

Evan had got up early and the fire was glowing in the range the delicious aroma of goose slowly roasting filled the room. Megan and Evan wrapped the children up in warm clothes to visit Margaret and William. They walked briskly up the hill, Evan carrying Dafydd and Megan carrying Bron. It was a bitterly cold morning and small flakes of snow were appearing on the horizon. Elizabeth
was positively glowing, pregnancy suited her, and she had been fortunate to remain healthy. Due to Elizabeth's condition, they were having dinner with Margaret and William. Once again Megan felt a tinge of longing for the organisation of Margaret's household but also looking forward to spending the rest of the day with her small families first Christmas dinner, which thankfully was a success, Megan, and Evan contentedly sat

looking at each other whilst the children had an afternoon nap. Their peace was disturbed by a knocking on the back door. They both exchanged a concerned glance to one another as nobody ever came to their back door.

They were both shocked and a little surprised to see Owen and Abigail accompanied by a small white dog. They hurried them into the safety of the cottage. Megan stood transfixed as she looked at Abigail, she could certainly see how Owen had been attracted to her she was indeed beautiful even though Megan had on her best Sunday dress she felt like a pauper when she looked at Abigail's outfit. She wore an emerald green skirt and cape and a pretty fur bonnet. The colour of her outfit reflected the colour of her eyes. When she removed her bonnet, it revealed a luxurious head of auburn hair. Abigail told them she had used the excuse that little Misty needed a walk hence the reason for their small companion. Despite their different circumstances Megan quickly took to Abigail she was not standoffish and posh like a lot of gentry Megan had met, but bubbly animated and full of life Megan's reservations about her attire and small home instantly fell away. Megan served tea and warm mince pies and they spent an enjoyable hour together. Megan was also surprised when Abigail gave her a hug and thanked her for welcoming her into their home, they both apologised for having to rush off but went on to explain Abigail had to get back before her excuse ran out.

Megan and Evan spent an enjoyable evening by the warm fireside playing with the children, enjoying their first Christmas in the comfort of their own home. It had been one of peace and tranquillity but made even more enjoyable by the arrival of Owen and Abigail. Megan could see how in love they both were but was fearful for Owen once he summoned up the courage to speak with Abigail's father. Megan prayed that Thomas Parry would see what a kind good natured man Owen was and accept him despite the differences in their stations in life.

CHAPTER SIX

Throughout January Megan had felt unwell, tired, dizzy and sick every morning she knew the signs but did not feel elated like she did when she was expecting Dafydd. It was the same feeling she experienced when she found out she was pregnant with Bron far too soon. She found it hard enough coping with Dafydd and Bron. Megan certainly did not feel ready for another baby. They were just starting to feel the benefit of Evan's extra income coming in every week. Megan did not feel ready to tell Evan about the news yet as she needed to address her emotions first and get used to the idea herself. Megan certainly did not want to end up like Lily Thomas next door, who had produced a baby every year for the past six years. Lily fortunately had a caring husband unlike poor Mair and her brood, also Lily's grandmother lived with the family. She was a robust woman fit and healthy who seemed to have more energy than most of the young mothers in the row of cottages. Megan knew if it wasn't for Lily's grandmother Lily would never have been able to cope on her own, goodness knows what would have happened to them if they were left totally in Lilys' care. Poor Lily was pleasant enough but awfully slow both physically and mentally. She always seemed as if her head was in the clouds.

Over the last couple of months Megan had got to know most of the families in the small row of cottages. She smiled to herself at the variety of families in such a small vicinity. Mair and her unruly brood resided at number two. Megan and Evan in number three and poor Lily and her ever increasing family resided next door. Then holy Joe as Evan had nicknamed Thomas at number one. It was only last month that Megan had become acquainted with the occupants of number five Mill Row.

It had been a particularly freezing morning and Megan was on her way to the shops. As she passed number five a tiny elderly lady stood on the doorstep, she smiled at Megan and greeted the children. She then went on to explain to Megan that her husband suffered from black lung disease which Megan knew was a common debilitating condition that was caused by coal dust after working for years underground. She asked Megan if she could call and see if Doctor Edwards could call on her husband as soon as possible as he was struggling to breathe. Megan inquired if there was anything else she could do to help Mrs Howells, but she simply thanked her and said she would go back inside and sit with her husband until the doctor arrived.

When Evan got home from work Megan left the children with him and went to see how Mr Howells was. Even though Mrs Howells said he was a lot better once the doctor had called Megan was quite distressed when she saw him. He was sitting on a chair by the fireside and simply nodded and smiled at Megan. His poor face was ashen, and his chest seemed to rattle as he struggled with every breath he took. She told them both she would call and see them the following day to see if there was anything they required. Mrs Howells thanked her and said it was lovely to have such a caring neighbour. She went on to explain that Mair had always looked after them. She had a great deal of admiration for Mair who even though everything in her life was chaotic, always made time to help anyone whenever she could.

Megan also felt resentment towards Rachel and Thomas they were supposed to be devout Christians but neither of them had the caring nature of Mair.

CHAPTER SEVEN

Megan lifted the basket of washing and took it outside to hang on the line. Even though it was a bright morning, there seemed to be dark clouds in the distance which appeared over the mountains behind Cefn. Due to the surrounding collieries the villagers were used to coal dust clouds, and specks of coal dust which unfortunately embedded themselves on the clothes hanging on the lines. Megan looked towards the mountain and the dark cloud appeared thicker and darker. It looked as if something was burning and drifting towards the village. Megan thought some trees had caught fire, then her heart thumped in her chest when she heard the sound every collier's wife dreads, the hooter going off at one of the nearby collieries heralding an accident at one of the nearby mines.

She ran outside and all the women in the street had gathered waiting to hear further news. They could see Mr Phillips cycling down Bedford Road on his rickety old bicycle, shouting to everyone he passed that there had been an accident at Cefn Slip. The women of Mill Row felt relieved to hear the accident had occurred at Cefn Slip Colliery. As all their husbands and sons were all employed at either Brynddu or Parc Slip. The sad news was that a timber prop had collapsed trapping several men in the mine. Nobody knew yet if there had been any loss of lives and everyone prayed the forthcoming news would be good.

Not a lot of housework was done in Mill Row that morning, as all the women sat on the small wall by the well gossiping over cups of tea, whilst the children run around playing enjoying their new found freedom. Megan knew by the look on Evan's face when he entered the cottage after work that evening that it was not good news. Five of the men had been severely injured and taken to a nearby hospital and there had sadly also been four fatalities, including thirteen-year-old Arwel Evans who lived in nearby Aberkenfig. This type of news always affected all the mining families as it brought home to them the danger, they faced everyday of their lives.

Megan had not been feeling well all day and she assumed it was the upset earlier this morning she was experiencing severe back pain and stomach cramps. It was past midnight and Evan worn out after a day's work was fast asleep beside her. Megan crept downstairs, each step more painful as she made her way to the bottom the cramps were becoming more severe and she felt a wetness between her legs, she slowly made her way outside to the toilets. Thankfully because it was the middle of the night nobody was about, she sat on the wooden bench in the toilet with her head bent forwards. She felt one last severe pain as a clot came away, she knew she was having a miscarriage and had lost the baby. Megan felt sick with remorse she had not wanted this baby and thought it was God's way of punishing her. She slowly walked back to the house feeling totally drained and exhausted she barely had the strength to lift the heavy kettle to place upon the stove to make some tea.

Megan sat alongside the dying embers and sipped the comforting warm tea. She must have drifted off to sleep when she awoke, she saw Evan standing there with a concerned expression on his face. Megan explained what had happened. Evan held her tightly as heart wrenching sobs shook her body. Evan knelt beside her and took her hands in his telling her it was not her fault or Gods punishment. It just was not meant to be. He said he would call into his mother's home on his way to the mine and ask if she would mind looking after the children so Megan could rest and regain her strength.

CHAPTER EIGHT

Unfortunately, Megan developed an infection after the miscarriage which brought on a fever. The doctor had suggested complete bed rest until Megan was fully recovered. For the next six weeks Margaret looked after Megan and the children. Mair also helped she always made extra food and brought it in for Margaret, Megan and the family. Rachel also helped, looking after the children. Sometimes she would sit by Megan's bed and read her passages from the Bible. Megan found it quite comforting as Rachel had a soft gentle voice which had a soothing effect on Megan. Even Dai pig's wife called in with bacon and fresh eggs for the children.

Whether it was due to the miscarriage; Megan had certainly not been feeling herself over the last couple of weeks she felt a strange sadness and all sorts of worrying thoughts seemed to be entering her mind. If someone had told Megan ten years ago that she would marry a miner and be living in the closely knit community of Cefn Cribbwr she would have laughed at them. This was certainly not the future she had envisaged for herself.

Megan had been born and raised in the nearby

seaside town of Porthcawl in the year 1864, her sister Amy was three years younger than her. Megan and Amy were privileged children for this era, as their father had never known unemployment and had been able to provide a comfortable life for his small family.

Megan's parents had been born in the nearby village of Pyle, a small hamlet situated between the seaside town of Porthcawl and the market town of Bridgend. They had been employed by Mr Talbot who owned the nearby Margam Estate. Her mother had worked there as a kitchen maid since she was twelve years old, and her father had been a stable boy. Over the years they had both been fortunate to work their way up in the household, her mother becoming a cook and her father a groom. The family looked after their staff and when Megan's parents married, they let them use the large kitchen to put on a spread for their family and friends. Unfortunately, after they were married there were no properties for her parents to live in on the estate and they were exceptionally fortunate to find a cottage in Philadelphia Road in Porthcawl. Her mother left her employment which was usual in those as people did not employ married women. For several years her father walked through the fields from Porthcawl to Margam come rain or shine. This took its toll on Megan's father as it was difficult in the cold and wet months. Even though he loved his job as a groom at the Margam Estate as he was getting older, he knew he could not continue the arduous walk to work every day.

CHAPTER NINE

Porthcawl in the early Nineteenth century consisted of two small Hamlets. Newton and Nottage. Then around 1845 railway mania arrived and steam engines replaced the horse drawn tramlines. In 1847 the Llynfi and Porthcawl Railway was formed. The railway system was really taking off around this time and a broad-gauge steam train started running from Maesteg to a junction with the South Wales line at Bridgend. Also, around the same time more broad-gauge rails were being laid to replace the tram road from Tondu to Porthcawl.

This was just the start of the small seaside town of Porthcawl being put on the map. It was all due to a businessman from Manchester John Brogden he had been attracted to South Wales by the mineral wealth that was now being mined in the area. He invested in the Tondu Ironworks and coal mining in the Ogmore Valley which was fast becoming a lucrative investment. In 1865 the Porthcawl Dock became the terminus for all the steam driven freight trains from both the Llynfi and Ogmore Valleys. The Brogdens were instrumental in obtaining an Act of Parliament for a huge development in the docks at Porthcawl.

Many people's lives have been changed thanks to John Brogden's construction and development of the docks in Porthcawl and the employment that ensued. Megan's father was just one of these grateful people. Megan's father loved his job as a groom at the Manor House, but the hours were long, and the pay was poor and walking there every day helped him make the big decision to leave. Many of his friends had left the farms where they had been employed as young boys and like many others were now employed at the docks in Porthcawl. The dockside area was a hive of activity; warehouses and store yards had been constructed near the wharfs and a row of cottages built nearby. This was originally called Company Row and it was now better known as Pilot Row.

He had started looking for work on the new breakwater and was fortunate enough to find employment there. So it was with a heavy heart that Megan's father bade farewell to Margam Manor and took up employment at the docks. He started working as a laborer working in the storehouse then working his way up to the more lucrative job in the ticket office.

This kind of life was a rarity, unemployment was rife in some areas. People were employed in the factories and woolen mills in the Midlands and northern England, but they worked long hours for very little pay and children as young as ten were employed in these areas. Megan had heard that children lived and begged on the streets in the City of London. Sanitation was so bad that death and disease were rife

To cater for the thirst of the new army of workers much to the disgust and dismay of the Temperance Society, public houses appeared to be springing up everywhere. The first being the Knights Arms then others followed in close succession. The General Picton, the Ship and Castle and the Harbor Inn.

Megan reflected on her early childhood years in Porthcawl, she remembered on warm summer evenings walking with her mother to meet her father from work. Megan loved these outings to her and Amy, the busy docks and breakwater was like a magical Kingdom. Watching the water lapping the sides of the huge container ships, the vast throngs of men loading and unloading the ships of their precious cargo. On several occasions if they timed it right and juicy oranges had arrived from some distant land one of the men would give them a wink and hand them an orange which was like receiving a precious jewel. Megan and Amy both got very excited to hear the steam train laden with coal pulling into the port. Then watching the men offloading the coal the dark dust dispersing into the atmosphere as they emptied the trams and transported the coal onto the waiting ships. Her favorite time was when her father had just received his pay packet and they would walk along the promenade towards Hattie's Ice Cream Parlor situated alongside the newly built Esplanade

Hotel. Megan and Amy would wait whilst her father purchased them delicious small ice cream cones and they would walk towards home slowly savoring their special treat.

Every Saturday the small family would walk to her grandmother's small cottage in the nearby village of Newton. The main thing Megan remembered was her grandmother's large garden full of beautiful flowers and vegetables. Megan sadly had never known her Grandfather as he had passed away when Megan was a baby.

Her Auntie Edith and Uncle Bertie resided with her grandmother. She loved Uncle Bertie who had unfortunately been born brain damaged and had the mind of a small child. He would run to the door and excitedly greet them jumping up and down then he would grasp the girls' hands and pull them upstairs to his bedroom ready to show them his latest project. Megan still had the small wooden doll he had given her. Every time they visited, they had to see the latest edition of his collection of shells he had gathered from the seashore.

His latest project was a paper kite he was making, and he promised Megan and Amy, he would finish it by next weekend and if the wind was right, they would go to Locks Common to fly it. Megan was a little afraid of Auntie Edith. She was in her late forties and had never
married. She told them her main love was Lord Jesus she very rarely joined in the conversation but instead sat in the large armchair reading her

Bible totally oblivious that there was ever anyone else in the room. Her Grandmother was a large sturdy woman she had a mop of unruly white hair and the most endearing smile. Even though her Grandmother was afflicted with arthritis she still managed to tend her garden with the help of Bertie and Edith. Megan's Grandmother was an amazing cook, and all the family looked forward to their visits to enjoy whatever fare she had prepared for them. Her Grandmother's pantry was a joy to behold, it contained shelves of various pickles and preserves. Nothing from the garden was ever wasted one thing Megan remembered was her Grandndmothers delicious bread spread thickly with homemade damson jam. Just thinking about it made Megan's mouth water. Megan and Amy loved to play hide and seek with Uncle Bertie in the large garden, he had also installed a homemade swing and they spent many a happy afternoon all taking it in turns to push each other back and forth.

During the winter months they would play indoor board games. As a child Saturday was Megan's favorite day. Her and Amy hated Sundays. They had to get up early in the morning and all the family went to the Chapel. Then Megan and Amy helped her mother prepare the vegetables for Sunday dinner. Her grandmother, Uncle Bertie and Aunt Edith would arrive, and dinner was served promptly at 1:00 o'clock. Her grandmother always brought one of her delicious homemade tarts made from whatever fruit she had picked from her garden.

The worst part for Megan and Amy was clearing the table after dinner and washing the mountains of dishes, pots, and pans that had accumulated. Whilst the adults sat and relaxed in the living room. Then at six o'clock the family would all leave for the evening service in Chapel.

Then when they got home it was bath night and the family took turns to use the old tin bath. Oh, how Megan hated Sundays, such a boring day with no fun to be had.

Megan and Amy were very privileged children, a new church school had recently been established in Newton village and because her Aunt Edith was a friend of the Minister who ran the school, they were both able to attend. There were only 20 pupils of various age groups in attendance. Amy was not too keen on learning, but Megan loved it. They were very fortunate children as they had both been taught to read and write, which once again was a rarity for the Nineteenth century.

Megan felt so grateful for her idyllic childhood, so many happy memories of the hours she spent enjoying the plentiful supply of golden sandy beaches that Porthcawl had to offer. Sadly, childhood days were short lived. Once children reached the age of ten, they were sent to work to help supplement the family's income as money was scarce and there were no laws regarding the exploitation of children.

Some of the factories and woolen mills in England employed children as young as eight and many a young life had been lost due to industrial accidents. There was no such thing as Health and Safety Laws to protect the workers. The only thing employers were concerned with was making large sums of money for themselves without a thought for their employees' welfare. If families became sick or unable to work, they were sent to the workhouse and for many poor families that's where they sadly lived the rest of their lives. Many died through overwork, malnutrition and the various diseases such as cholera and diphtheria.

Young boys and girls were employed in the coal mines working long arduous shifts and very rarely seeing daylight. It was heartbreaking for mothers to see their young children accompanying their fathersas they set out for their long day down the mine. Other children were lucky they were employed on the farms and even though their hours were long, they were well fed and healthy as they worked outdoors. Between the ages of twelve and fourteen many young girls went into service in the large houses in various parts of the country. Once again, the work was hard and the hours long and if there were no houses nearby girls were sent to other parts of the country to work. They were only allowed home to see their families once a month.

CHAPTER TEN

Megan still recalled the day she walked nervously along the long stretch of promenade towards the Brogden's large house which stood majestically looking out towards the Bristol Channel. Her mother walked alongside her to give her moral support and advice on what to say. Megan had never seen such a large imposing property and could not believe only one family lived there. They slowly walked around the house to the servants' quarters at the back of the building. Megan's mother told her not to be nervous as the butler showed her inside. Thankfully the housekeeper who introduced her was friendly and this made Megan feel at ease.

After what seemed like hours Megan was told she had the job of scullery maid and would start work promptly at six am next Monday, she was handed her uniform and shown back through the door. Megan's mother was waiting anxiously outside to see how she had got on and was delighted that she was going to be employed there as Megan would be able to live at home and walk the short distance to work every day.

Both Megan and her mother breathed a large sigh of relief and knew how fortunate she had been as local jobs in service were scarce.

Megan was pleased but she also felt sad because her best friend Annie who lived next door had not been able to find any employment in Porthcawl or the surrounding countryside and was going to travel to the West Country to work. Poor Annie was a nervous soul and Megan didn't know how she was going to cope being away from home, Megan just wished her, and Annie could have both found work in the Brogden's household.

There were many tears shed when Annie left the small seaside town for pastures new, but for Megan and Annie it would seem like an eternity before Annie would be able to come home for a visit.

Megan's first day at work was one she would never forget. She just wished she could have continued with her schooling and gone on to become a governess, but that unfortunately was not meant to be.

Even after all these years Megan's heart missed a beat when she remembered her employment at the Brogden household. All the staff were kind, but the work was so hard. A scullery maid's job entailed doing all the menial tasks washing and scrubbing floors, cleaning large cooking vessels, peeling vegetables, black leading all the extremely large grates in the house, a task she hated most of all.

Lizzie who was fourteen years old and had worked for the Brogdens for two years explained to Megan that she started doing the same job and if Megan worked hard and did not complain over the next couple of years, she would be able to work her way up the ladder and the work would be easier. Lizzie was now kitchen maid, and the cook was showing her various new skills, she said even though she had to clean and do vegetables the work was now more interesting and enjoyable, she told Megan just to be patient. Megan remembered going home completely exhausted for the first couple of months, but when she felt upset and angry about how her life had changed, she thought of poor Annie all alone in the big house in the West Country.

Megan remembered the good times as well as the bad times at work. She recalled the one occasion when the Brogdens had decided to host a summer ball. Megan had found that evening particularly enjoyable, after all the hard work and food preparation had been completed, herself, Lizzie and Mrs Brogdens lady's maid went to the upstairs bedroom and watched the carriages driving up outside the house. It was certainly a sight to behold all the gentlemen in their finery and the ladies in their beautiful ball gowns. Once they had entered the house the girls quickly but quietly ran from the bedroom to the top of the staircase where they hid discreetly and were able to watch the ladies' cloaks being removed to reveal the various colors and styles of their ballgowns. After the guests had eaten and everything had been cleared away all the staff assembled around the large kitchen table chatting about the evening's event and partaking of what was left over from the sumptuous feast that the cook had prepared The Brogdens were good employers and looked after their staff and over the next couple of years Megan went from scullery maid to kitchen maid.

CHAPTER ELEVEN

If only life had carried on like this Megan would have been quite content. Unfortunately, when Megan was fifteen there was a severe outbreak of diphtheria in the small seaside town of Porthcawl. It was believed to have originated from someone who had worked on one of the large container ships at the docks. It started with a few of the dockers and their families but quickly spread like wildfire.

An endless stream of tears flowed down Megan's cheeks. This had been such a dark period in her life. She remembered her father coming home from work on a cold November evening. He had a sallow complexion and was complaining of a sore throat, over the next couple of days he developed a fever and even though her mother had tried to remain positive and nursed him day and night after ten days he succumbed to diphtheria which took his life. Sadly, Amy had also contracted it and within seven days she had passed away. Even though both Megan and her mother both felt unwell they nursed her Grandmother, Uncle Bertie and Aunty Edith.

Megan awoke one morning. She felt so unwell she struggled to get out of bed, but she knew she must help her mother nurse the family as best she could. She felt so cold and could not stop shivering she wrapped her dressing gown around her and walked downstairs to her Grandmother's kitchen.

As she approached the bottom of the stairs, she heard a thump. Her heart missed a beat, and her worst fears were realized when she saw her mother lying on the floor. She dragged herself towards her and carefully lifted her onto the nearby chair. Her mother's face was pale, and beads of perspiration were on her face and neck. She felt hot to touch. Megan wrapped a blanket around her and went next door to Mrs Davis. Poor Mrs Davis had also suffered during this epidemic. She had lost six of her ten children and her husband's health was deteriorating. Mrs Davis told Megan that Doctor Thomas was on his way as there were several people in the small row of houses who had taken a turn for the worse, she told Megan to go back into the warm to look after the family and she would send the doctor in as soon as he arrived. Megan's mother was sleeping when she got back in, but her breathing was labored, and Megan feared the worst. Aunt Edith came downstairs. This was the first time in Megan's life that she had seen Auntie Edith show any emotion. She held Megan and Megan recalled how weak and frail her body felt. Deep sobs racked her body as she said her Grandmother and Uncle Bertie had passed away during the night.

Aunt Edith insisted Megan go back to bed as she

could see she was also on the verge of collapse. Auntie Edith told Megan not to worry, she would look after her mother until the doctor arrived. For the next two weeks Megan remembered Aunt Edith tirelessly caring for her, mopping her brow, changing her sweat soaked nightdress and feeding her broth, but Megan felt no wish to recover after hearing the news that her mother had also passed away two days ago. She now felt as if she had lost the will to live, but God had other plans.

CHAPTER TWELVE

It was a long slow process six months have now passed and Megan and Aunt Edith had now regained their strength. After all they had been through Megan had now become closer to Aunt Edith.

Due to Megan's long road to recovery, she had lost her employment at the Brogden household. Thanks to Aunt Edith over the past couple of months she had started helping in the small village school. Her confidence had grown, and it had given her something to focus on. Megan now lived in Newton Village with Aunt Edith and a completely new life had now emerged. Aunt Edith had now become Headmistress at Newton school and they both shared the household chores and the upkeep of the large garden.

Megan wasn't the happy-go-lucky child she once was, and she experienced dark periods when she missed her family. It also helped Megan that they weren't the only ones learning to live with their grief. Many families had been wiped out during the diphtheria epidemic. Aunt Edith was a changed person, she was no longer trapped in her own small world, she had somehow through all the tragedies become a stronger, more caring person. She was a stalwart of the community and regularly visited families in need. Megan would often accompany her on these visits.

Another major milestone in Megan's life was when she had started attending chapel with Aunt Edith. The new chapel she went to was so different to what she had been used to in the past. Aunt Edith had never forced her to go to Hope Chapel with her but for Megan this was a new kind of religion, they called themselves nonconformists. Instead of having the same Minister speaking every Sunday every couple of weeks a new preacher would be present some from as far afield as West Wales where a new kind of religious revival was starting to emerge. There was more of a community spirit in the Chapel and Pastor Caradog Morgan who had a great love of music, had formed a Choral Society which Megan and Aunt Edith were part of.

The minister of the Chapel was also interested in the children's educational needs that for so long had been neglected.

During this period of her life Megan had made new friends in the Chapel and threw herself into every aspect of Chapel life, as well as the Choral Society she helped teach the small Sunday School which had grown considerably over the last couple of months.

Another reason for the change in Aunt Edith was her friendship with Caradog Morgan, Megan smiled to herself when she remembered the time she had realized her aunt's infatuation with Caradog. She had never been a vain person and in the past had never had any interest in her appearance, but over the last couple of weeks Megan had noticed her buying new material to make herself a new dress for Sunday and she had also purchased a new bonnet to wear.

CHAPTER THIRTEEN

Megan had just turned seventeen and it had been two long years since she had lost her family, she still had bad days and many a night she had cried herself to sleep when she thought of all she had lost.

Megan was sitting in the garden one warm summers evening in July she savored the warmth of the sunshine, as she sat there enjoying her sewing, her thoughts were interrupted as she heard the front door opening Aunt Edith came through the house and into the garden like a whirlwind, Megan was quite taken aback by the sudden turn of events. She put her sewing aside and gave her aunt her undivided attention. She appeared to be quite flushed, and her face was bright red. Aunt Edith sat down beside Megan and excitedly told her there was going to be a church convention in Penygroes a small village in West Wales, she explained there would be a large marquee on the village green and several churches would be attending, consisting of the Pentecostal, Baptist, Methodist and their own church groups. Megan simply nodded then she realized why Aunt Edith was so excited, she told Megan that Pastor

Caradog had asked them to accompany him in his pony and trap. She told Megan it would be in two weeks' time so they would need to get busy and make a new outfit each for the event and they also needed to sort out what food they would need to take.

Megan didn't think Aunt Edith had slept much the night before she must have been ready at least two hours before Pastor Caradog was due to pick them up. Megan herself also felt excited at the prospect of such an event.

Pastor Caradog was his usual punctual self and arrived promptly at 7:30 am. This was Megan's first experience of a ride in a pony and trap, she found it a very enjoyable experience jaunting along at a steady pace. The sun was shining, which only added to her enjoyment.

It certainly was a sight to behold when they arrived. The Marquee was huge. Large throngs of people were gathered laughing and chatting to each other. Several banners had been staked into the ground around the marquee, they were gently swaying in the warm breeze. The banners had been lovingly made each giving a different message of praise, God is love, Jesus Saves, Behold the King to name just a few.

Megan had never experienced anything like this before and found the atmosphere electric. People she had never seen before came up and hugged her and kissed her on the cheek children were running around enjoying their freedom away from the watchful eyes of their parents. A young girl named Betsy walked towards Megan and Edith and asked them if they would like to meet people from her local church who had arranged this event. Pastor Caradog had excused himself as he explained he needed a quiet place to contemplate his sermon that he was preaching later that evening.

Once again Megan was in awe of everything that had been prepared for the event. Betsy took them to the nearby church hall, Megan had never seen such a display of food, it had all been laid out on long trestle tables, with adequate seating around the large church hall. She poured them both a refreshing glass of homemade lemonade which they both thirstily drank down. Her Aunt placed her wares onto the table as all the other church members had done previously. Aunt Edith started chatting happily away to some members of the Baptist Church who she hadn't seen for a few years.

Whilst Megan was chatting to Betsy, she noticed two young boys walking into the hall, they were both very handsome but certainly did not appear comfortable in their Sunday best suits, both pulling at their collars as if they were too tight on their necks. They walked towards Betsy and Megan then introduced themselves as Evan and Owen Roberts. Megan was surprised to find out that they had also travelled some distance to get there, they explained they only lived about 5 miles away from Megan and her aunt. They resided in a small village called Cefn Cribbwr. Megan smiled and explained she had never ventured further than Porthcawl or Newton. They said they were both miners and worked in the local colliery. Megan and Betsy had both become so absorbed in the conversation with the boys they had not realized the time until Betsy's mother called them to explain that the day's events were now starting in the marquee, both Megan and Betsy reluctantly followed Betsy's mother out of the church hall with the young men following closely behind.

It had been a long time since Megan had felt this happy, it was wonderful to see so many people gathered singing, praying and listening to the short sermons the various preachers from the different churches gave. She enjoyed chatting to new people in the church hall afterwards and enjoyed the wonderful food on offer, she did not want the day to end. The only sad part was saying goodbye to the two brothers they had met earlier. When she arrived home for the first time in two years, she put her head on her pillow when she went to bed and closed her eyes and slept soundly.

CHAPTER FOURTEEN

For the next couple of weeks Megan could not stop thinking about Evan. Then as if her prayers had been answered Pastor Caradog called to the house and said he was preaching in Siloam Chapel in Cefn on Sunday and would Edith and Megan like to accompany him. Megan had to curtail herself and did not dare show her aunt or the Pastor how excited she was. As she lay in bed that night, she told herself not to have foolish thoughts Cefn was probably a large place and had many chapels and churches and the likelihood of her seeing Evan was non-existent.

Sunday evening arrived and Megan had made an extra effort with her appearance just in case. Cefn Cribbwr was a lot smaller than Megan had been expecting in fact it wasn't much bigger than Newton Village. Siloam Chapel was a very impressive large building. It stood majestically on the top of a steep hill with a small row of houses below it and the rest of the village opposite it. As Caradog was preaching they arrived quite early so sat in the front of the Chapel. Megan did try and turn around once or twice to see if she could catch sight of Evan but decided to give up and just enjoy the service and Caradog's sermon.

Various people stopped to talk to Pastor Caradog and her aunt, so Megan made her way out of the Chapel to wait for them. Just as she approached the doorway someone tapped her on the shoulder. Her heart missed a beat, and she could feel the color rising in her cheeks when she saw Evan standing there smiling at her. They chatted for a while then Megan got a little embarrassed when she could see her aunt and the Pastor approaching. Evan introduced himself explaining they had met each other at the church convention in Penygroes. They both seemed quite taken with the pleasant young man. Evan then introduced them to his family. and asked if they would like to go back to his Parent's house for tea and cake. Megan held her breath waiting for answers she had her fingers crossed tightly behind her back secretly chanting to herself "please say yes." Much to Megan's delight they both agreed. Megan walked down the hill with Evan and his brother Owen. Whilst her aunt and the Pastor walked behind with Evans parents and his other brother Bryn and sister-in-law Elizabeth, Evan's mother appeared aloof, but his father was very pleasant, they all chatted and enjoyed a refreshing cup of tea and some of his mother's homemade fruitcake. One thing you could be certain of there was never any shortage of conversion when you were in the presence of Pastor Caradog.

    Megan didn't want the afternoon to end she just wanted to spend time with Evan but all too quickly the time came for them to leave. Evan approached her aunt and enquired if it would be amicable for him to visit Megan next Saturday which was his day off. Thankfully, her aunt agreed and said they would look forward to seeing him.

The days dragged on for Megan until at long Saturday arrived. Megan tried not to run to answer the door, simply trying to be calm and demure. Her Aunt was kind enough to make herself scarce to enable Megan and Evan to enjoy their time together. Evan explained that he had been fortunate and hadn't had to walk from Cefn, he said he managed to get a ride on the Coal train, which was going to the break water, he told Megan he had never heard of Newton so had to ask for directions. They spent a wonderful afternoon in the garden chatting to each other, then Evan joined Megan and her aunt for afternoon tea. Unfortunately, the afternoon just flew by before he left Evan asked Aunt Edith for her permission to court Megan. Once again, she agreed to his request.

Whenever Evan had a day off from the mine, he would spend the day with Megan. They loved walking hand in hand along the promenade weather permitting on a few occasions when Pastor Caradog was preaching in Siloam, they were invited to join Evans family for Sunday dinner.

The next two years were the happiest Megan had known since her parents and sister had passed away. Megan and Evan had fallen in love and wanted to spend every minute together. Megan was brimming over with excitement as Aunt Edith had given her permission for them to get married.

CHAPTER FIFTEEN

Saturday the 5th of September had finally arrived Megan and Evans' wedding day. She awoke early and felt a mixture of excitement and apprehension, especially after the long discussion she had had with her aunt last month. Aunt Edith had explained to Megan that marriage was a big commitment and not something to be taken lightly, she told Megan life would be very different when she was married and became a miner's wife. It would be hard work cooking and cleaning and taking care of children once they came along, she told her even though she had Evan and his family it would be a great change moving to a mining community in Cefn Cribbwr and no longer living near the seaside in Porthcawl.

Megan had never been a headstrong girl and she had listened carefully and mulled over her aunt's kindly advice. Aunt Edith had tried to persuade her to wait another couple of years before committing to marriage but as soon as she saw Evan and they spent time together she knew she really wanted to be with him no matter how hard the consequences were. She pushed all negative thoughts to the back of her mind. Megan's thoughts were interrupted by a knock on the door which heralded arrival of

Pastor Caradog. Megan hugged him affectionately when she saw what he had done. His pony and trap was decorated with pretty flowers and white ribbons.

Megan and her aunt sat proudly alongside him as they made the short journey to Hope Chapel. Aunt Edith took her seat in the front of the Chapel whilst Megan waited until it was time for Pastor Caradog to walk her down the aisle. Megan could feel a lump in her throat and tears filled her eyes wishing it was her father alongside her and her family sitting together happily in the front of the Chapel. As the music played and she walked towards the front of the church her thoughts dispersed when she saw Evan proudly standing there in his Sunday best suit.

As the weather was good members from the Chapel had erected a large tent on Newton Green for her wedding breakfast and small tables and chairs were placed outside it. Today had been a bittersweet sweet day for Megan everything had been perfect but there was an ache in her heart thinking of her beloved parents and sister Amy.

Aunt Edith had kindly offered to spend two nights with her friends to enable Megan and Evan to spend their short honeymoon at the cottage. Megan remembered looking deeply into Evans' eyes as evening came and they walked hand in hand towards Primrose Cottage. Evan and Megan sat on the small wooden bench looking down on the beautiful garden, once again she could feel tears pricking her eyes as she remembered her grandmother and Uncle Bertie busily weeding the garden. As if to intercept her thoughts Evan squeezed her hand. They sat there enjoying the late evening sun and reminiscing about their perfect wedding day. Evan explained to Megan he had lots of concerns he needed to discuss with her. He said he would love to give her a home like her aunt's small cottage, but unfortunately the miners' cottages certainly were not anything like this. He also told her he was worried about her leaving her life behind and giving up the job she loved and moving to a small mining community where life was going to be totally different. Evan then apologized that they would have to live with his parents until a home of their own became available. He said another of his concerns was his mother. Evan said she was not an easy person to get along with and asked Megan to try and be patient with her. Megan hugged Evan and told him she had thought about all the matters concerned and she knew she would be homesick for Porthcawl, but he was not to worry, she was simply happy to be his wife and see him every day.

Megan also told Evan he could always apply for a job at the break water and then they would be able to live in Porthcawl. Evan did not want to disappoint Megan and found it easier just to agree with her. He did not want to worry her but knew deep down he would always work in the mine like his father and brothers. They spent the last day of their honeymoon having a nice lay in and strolling along the promenade. The weather was good, so they sat on a large rock looking out to sea and enjoyed the sandwiches Megan had prepared. They walked back to Newton and sat outside the Ancient Britain Public House, Evan enjoying a pint of cold beer and Megan a refreshing lemonade. It had started to rain in the evening, so they sat at the large kitchen table and enjoyed a casserole that Megan had prepared last night.

CHAPTER SIXTEEN

The two blissful days they had spent at the cottage passed far too quickly. Megan woke on Monday morning feeling anxious and a little nauseous. Suddenly reality had now hit her and all the trouble thoughts she had pushed to the back of her mind were now emerging. She could not hold back her emotions when Aunt Edith arrived. The tears flowed slowly down her cheeks when the time came to say goodbye to her beloved hometown and move on to pastures new. She pulled herself together for Evans's sake as they made the journey to Cefn Cribbwr.

As she walked through the front door of Evans' parents' house, she tried to block all thoughts from her mind. The stark reality suddenly hit her. Evan was right, her unfamiliar environment was a complete contrast to the one she had left behind.

A week after Megan had moved into Evans' parents' cottage, she received the devastating news that Aunt Edith had sadly had a massive stroke and passed away.

Megan spent the first three months of her marriage trying to persuade Evan to look for a job at the breakwater in Porthcawl. Evan knew Megan was homesick and missing Porthcawl, so he was very patient with her, telling her he was thinking about it. Megan knew she had made the right decision marrying Evan he was a kind and considerate husband and had been so understanding with her he knew what a big transition it had been to her way of life. Things would have been different if her mother-in-law was a compassionate woman and understood Megan's immaturity but that was not in her nature.

Evan waited until Megan was expecting their first child to tell her that he had no desire to move to Porthcawl and work on the breakwater. He told her he understood her concerns, he knew what a difficult life it was being a miner's wife, living in constant fear for his safety underground. He told her the days were long and the work was hard, but he couldn't envisage himself doing any other kind of work. Megan told him she understood and promised him she wouldn't mention him looking for work or moving to Porthcawl She told him she was starting to adjust to her new way of life in the mining community and there were so many unhappy memories for her in Porthcawl that she now knew it was time to move on, and hopefully by the time the baby arrived they would have a home of their own.

Her past now seemed so long ago. Her contented childhood in the small seaside town of Porthcawl. Then the devastating loss of her family. and the new life of contentment she eventually found with

Aunt Edith. So many memories good and bad. The feeling of homesickness now started to dissipate, and Megan's thoughts reflected on all the good things she now had. A wonderful husband, two beautiful children and a home of their own finally.

CHAPTER SEVENTEEN

Megan was so grateful to have such wonderful caring neighbours. After four weeks Megan was starting to regain her strength, but Margaret insisted on helping until she was fully recovered. It was a good job Margaret was such a strong woman as Elizabeth's baby was due the end of March and she also had to look after William who was suffering from bronchitis, it was the first time in over 10 years that he had not been well enough to go down the mine. So poor Margaret was devoting her time to looking after them both.

March also saw sadness ascend on the little row of houses. Poor Mr Howells had finally succumbed to the black lung disease and passed away. Megan was upset that she had not been well enough to attend the funeral. The first thing she would do as soon as she was well enough was visit Mrs Howells.

The year of 1891 had certainly not started well for the families of Mill Row and the unfortunate families of Aberkenfig after the tragedy at Cefn Colliery.

Beautiful sunshine heralded the arrival of April. Megan was now fully recovered and looking forward to going walking once again with the children.

As she opened the front door, his spirits were lifted on the grass verge opposite the small row of cottages beautiful daffodils now appeared in full bloom. They reared their trumpet shaped heads to greet the warmth of the spring sunshine.

Whilst Megan had been recuperating, she had wild away the hours making gifts. She had made two pretty bonnets for Mair and Rachel and knitted two shawls one for Margaret and one for Rachel.

It felt so good to finally escape the confines of her tiny cottage. Margaret was delighted to see Megan and the children. Megan was quite taken aback when Margaret hugged her when she gave her the shawl. Could it be that Margaret's dour nature was mellowing with the passing years.

Megan went over to give William a hug he said he now felt stronger, and his cough was subsiding. He told her he was not relishing the thought of going back down to the mine in two days' time, but sadly if he was unable to work there was no money coming in and they had nearly used all their rainy-day money they had put aside. Megan was about to leave when Elizabeth arrived. She said she had been awake most of the night with back ache. Megan and Margaret exchanged knowing glances it seemed like they would be having a new member in the Roberts' household over the next day or so.

Megan knocked on Mrs Howell's door on her

way back home, there was no answer, so Megan assumed she was out shopping. Megan could not believe how exhausted she felt she had only walked the short distance to Bedford Road and back. She decided to postpone her visit to Mair and Rachel and go in a day or two.

Megan had decided while she had some energy, she would bake some bread and prepare broth for their evening meal. The children had been exceptionally good this morning which enabled Megan to get some chores done. Megan was preparing the bath for Evan when there was a knock on the door. As soon as she opened it and saw Margaret standing there smiling, she knew what the news was. Margaret announced that William Bryn Roberts had arrived. A healthy 8 pound 3 ounces, she was also pleased to report that both mother and baby were doing well. Megan felt quite emotional it was such a joy to have good news for a change, it had certainly been a difficult couple of months. Evan was overjoyed at the news and looking forward to this evening when he would be visiting the White Lion with Bryn and Owen to wet the baby's head. Megan was already asleep when she heard Evan trying to close the door and creep up the stairs. Megan could tell he was a little worse for wear. Unlike Mair's husband Evan was an incredibly happy drunk he fell into bed besides Megan pleasantly chuckling to himself. Then preceded to fall asleep as soon as his head touched the pillow. Evan was unaccustomed to drinking alcohol and Megan had to wake him for work. Not long after Evan left for work Dafydd and Bron were both awake. Megan told them both they were going to visit their new baby cousin later. Dafydd was extremely excited, but Bron looked a little confused.

Megan was surprised at how well Elizabeth looked. Elizabeth was sitting up in bed gazing lovingly at young William, she looked so proud. Megan felt so pleased for Elizabeth she knew how much she had longed for this moment. After visiting Elizabeth Megan then called in to see Mair and gave her the bonnet she had made. Mair was overjoyed to receive it. Poor Mair did not receive many gifts. The children had a wonderful time running around the tiny room into the scullery then out into the yard. All the children chasing each other and laughing together. It was always a pleasure to visit Mair even though her small brood of children were unruly they were a contented bunch.

Before going home Megan called in to see Rachel with her gift. Rachel was also delighted with her bonnet. She then made them both a cup of tea. Rachel gave the children a large piece of cake which kept them both quiet whilst Megan and Rachel chatted. Rachel was keen to hear the news about Elizabeth's baby. When Megan got back to her cottage, she felt exhausted it had been an extremely busy morning visiting everyone. She made a mental note to call and see Mrs Howells again towards the end of the week. Now all her visiting had been completed and the weather was getting warmer Megan was looking forward to taking the children to the Waun for a walk and a picnic. Megan's miscarriage and long recovery period had certainly put things into perspective. She now felt more content and looked forward to each new day. Another of the reasons for her wellbeing was Evan had now settled well into his new employment at Parc Slip. Evan and Megan had also heard the news that Owen had been to visit Abigail Parry's father. The outcome was certainly one that they had not been expecting. Mr Parry had told Owen he had reservations for his daughter's future with Owen, but then went on to explain how he had seen Owen mature from a 14-year-old boy at Brynddu to the responsible man he was now. Another factor he had considered was his respect for William, who had been a diligent miner all his life and had brought his three sons up to respect people.

Owen told Evan and Megan at the end of Mr Parry's speech, he shook Owen's hand, then preceded to tell him if he ever let Abigail down in anyway Owen would have him to answer to him and he would be a deeply sorry man. His parting words to Owen were "look after my daughter show her the love and respect, she deserves and please do not betray my trust in you boy".

After all the joyous news over the last couple of weeks Mill Row was once again tinged with sadness to hear the news that Mrs Howells had sadly passed away. Her son who resided in the Midlands said his mother had never fully recovered after his father's death. He said she had nursed him for over 10 years with the black lung disease, and when he was no longer with her, she seemed unable to cope being on her own. It was as if her main purpose in life had been taken from her and she started to neglect herself, she had not bothered to cook for herself and had become weaker every day. Her son said he had tried desperately for her to go and live with him in the Midlands, but she would not leave her home.

Nearly all the village of Cefn turned out for Mrs Howells funeral. The small chapel was full, and people were standing outside. The families of Mill Row organised the food and everyone went back to the Village Hall afterwards. Her son said his parents would have been so happy to see how loved they had been.

CHAPTER EIGHTEEN

Megan was feeling back to full strength now and looking forward to her walking with the children. With the arrival of May there was some warmth in the air. Sunlight filtered through the small window panes. Megan decided today she would do her first visit of the year to the Waun. She wrapped the pieces of bread and jam into a cloth feeling confident as it was early May there would be no wasps around to be attracted to the sweetness of the jam. She filled her small container with some fresh water from the well and set off.

As she approached the small thicket surrounding the Waun, she was perturbed to hear noises in the distance. Normally the only sounds she would hear would be the chirping of the birds in the trees and hedgerows. Megan tentatively walked towards the opening to the Waun. The closer she got the louder the noises. She could hear a multitude of voices, dogs barking loudly and what appeared to be small clouds of smoke slowly ascending towards the sky. As Megan got closer to the clearing, she was horrified at the scene in front of her eyes. She grabbed Dafydd's hand and hoisted Bron onto her hip to stop them running into the carnage that was her once peaceful Waun.

Travellers had invaded it.

There were about six brightly coloured wooden caravans and homemade dwellings. These consisted of large sheets of tarpaulin roped across several of the trees. It was a hive of activity. Large groups of children running around dogs barking some fighting amongst themselves others happily playing together. Women sitting on the small step ladders leading into the caravans. She could see several men in the distance brushing down horses. Also, men were repairing or making a hand cart. Pots were boiling on the small groups of open fires around the site.

Megan stood transfixed at the scene in front of her. She turned to walk back before someone saw her. As she turned around, she bumped into a man who had obviously been watching her. She was terrified as she felt she had been intruding and he was going to harm her.

Megan could not have been more mistaken. The man in front of her gave her a beaming smile and simply said "hello my pretty lady where have you come from". Megan was speechless. He had a very pleasant look about him. His red hair poked out from under his cap. His eyes were an unusual bluey green colour. Around his neck he wore a brightly coloured scarf. His shirt was open at the neck showing his muscular body. His brown corduroy trousers were tied at the waist with twine and tucked into his muddy boots.

Megan felt the need to apologise. She explained

she always brought the children here when the weather was agreeable. Feeling embarrassed Megan just wanted to walk away. As she turned to leave the man took hold of her hand and shook it, he introduced himself as Patrick O'Leary or better known to his friends as Paddy. Megan could feel the colour rising in her cheeks as he winked at her and exclaimed "you can call me Paddy". Megan still felt angry and saddened that her haven had been invaded. Paddy apologised to Megan for frightening her. He then went on to explain they had arrived from Ireland a week ago and set up camp. He said life in Ireland had become desperate over the last couple of years. Their crops of potatoes had been hit by blight destroying their livelihood and existence. Many of the rich landowners had not been sympathetic to the poor farmers of Ireland and instead of helping them had evicted many families. He said that starvation and typhoid had been rife. Many people had now fled Ireland and were continuing to do so at an alarming rate. He said his brother and his family had emigrated to America to try and make a better life for themselves. Paddy then went on to explain a lot of his fellow Irish loved the freedom of the open road and not being stuck in one place. He said they travelled the country looking for work. They had heard that there was plenty of work in the Welsh valleys due to the start of the iron industry and coal mining. Megan knew there were many Welsh families living in poverty but felt this was nothing compared to the way people had suffered in Ireland.

She suddenly felt a kindred spirit in Paddy. Megan was about to return home when Paddy asked her if the children would like to see the horses and some puppies. Megan was about to decline his offer when Dafydd in his usual excited way started jumping up and down shouting "please mam can we please". Poor Dafydd had been so patient tenderly holding her hand while she had been listening to Paddy. She thought it would be cruel to deny his small request. Paddy said he would introduce her to his sister Colleen. Megan looked straight ahead as she nervously walked through the campsite, she could sense everyone's eyes upon her. Paddy introduced her to Colleen. She had the same colouring as Paddy, but her eyes were a deep green. Her long hair was covered by a brightly coloured scarf. Megan felt quite envious of the clothes she wore. The shawl she had draped around her shoulders was black with bright red flowers on it and it was edged with a red lace fringe. Her skirt was black and made of a beautiful silk material. In contrast to her outfit, she appeared to be wearing black Wellington boots. Paddy suggested Megan had a cup of tea with Colleen while he took the children to see the ponies and puppies.

Megan felt anxious as she had never met anyone like Colleen before and did not know what to say to her. Colleen instantly made Megan feel at home. She made her a cup of tea from the kettle that had been boiling on the open fire. Coleen explained they lived in a close-knit community and did not really bother with outsiders as they travelled around the country so much. Megan felt guilty when Colleen said they were not welcome in most places as people felt they were intruders and taking work they were not entitled to. The time passed quickly as both women shared their totally different lifestyles. When Paddy arrived back with the children Megan did not want to leave. There was something exciting about the travellers and their way of life. Paddy accompanied Megan back to the clearing at the edge of the campsite and bid her farewell, then with his mischievous grin he once again winked at her, and said she was welcome to visit again anytime.

Megan walked back across the fields with the children where she found a nice sunny spot for them to have their picnic. Dafydd was very animated he did not stop talking about the horses and puppies. The children ran around chasing each other whilst Megan relaxed on the grass. She did not know what it was but her meeting with the travellers had stirred something deep inside her, it was a kind of restlessness. Megan now felt her life to be boring and mundane compared to Colleen's. For some reason as she walked towards home, she did not want to tell Evan about her adventure today somehow, she knew he would not approve but she was certainly not prepared for how cross he would be when he found out.

CHAPTER NINETEEN

Evan had barely walked through the cottage door when Dafydd ran towards him excitedly telling him everything that had happened that morning. Evan glared at Megan then preceded to fling his cap onto the floor. In all the years they had been married Megan had never seen Evan so angry. He asked her what an earth had possessed her to go into a traveller's camp with a stranger she did not know. He said did she understand how dangerous these people were. Before Megan had chance to answer Evan slammed his fist on the table small particles of coal dust from his jacket drifted into the air. Megan felt the need to defend these people and explain how hard their life had been in Ireland, but somehow, she knew if she did it would only make matters worse. So begrudgingly she apologised to Evan then walked away to continue filling his bath. Evan apologised for losing his temper. He told Megan she was not to go anywhere near that campsite again. Evan started chatting over the dinner table making small talk regarding his day's work down the mine, but Megan was still angry. She felt Evans's outburst had destroyed all the pleasure she had gained from earlier today.

The following day she went to visit Elizabeth and the baby. Both families went for a walk together Elizabeth proudly pushing her pram up Bedford Road. Megan told Elizabeth about what had happened yesterday. Instead of taking Megan's side Elizabeth agreed with Evan and told Megan she must heed Evans's warning and not go near that place again it was far too dangerous. This put Megan back into a bad mood again.

Over the next two weeks Megan tried to put the traveller's campsite out of her mind she kept herself busy cleaning and baking.

Margaret called in unexpectedly and asked Megan if she could take the children out for the morning. Margaret told Megan she was looking a bit under the weather and having a bit of time to herself might lift her spirits. Megan was grateful and thanked Margaret and said she might have the opportunity without the children to get some cleaning done. After Margaret had left Megan was settling down to stitching together a small garment for Bron. The sunlight was shining through the small window pane and Megan was getting restless. She did not want to disobey Evan, but Paddy and Coleen had been so welcoming when she met them, she felt the need to explain why she had not kept her promise to visit them again and without the children Evan would never know.

She opened the door of her cottage and checked up and down the street thankfully nobody was about, so she briskly walked across the road and into the fields beyond. As she looked towards the Waun she could see someone in the distance foraging in the hedgerows. She was delighted as she got closer to find it was Colleen. When Coleen looked up and saw Megan, she came running towards her flinging her arms around Megan and kissing her gently on the cheek. Megan was so glad she had made the decision to return.

They walked into the campsite together. Coleen took her basket inside the caravan then preceded to make Megan a cup of tea. Megan was disappointed when Coleen said that most of the men had found work in the area including Paddy. She said they were loading the coal drams onto the trains for delivery to the breakwater at Porthcawl. Others had found work at the brickworks at nearby Tondu. Megan knew it was wrong, but she felt disappointed that she would not see Paddy. She explained to Colleen about her husband's disapproval of her visit. Being tactful and telling her he was wary of strangers, but Colleen threw her head back and laughed telling Megan not to worry about offending her they were used to being disliked by other people. Megan told Colleen she could not stay for long as she needed to get back home before her mother-in-law came back with the children. Coleen asked Megan if she could find another opportunity to visit as next Sunday evening was the 1st of June and all the travellers celebrated the start of summer with music and dancing. Megan said she would love to come but could not promise anything, but she would try her best.

Megan had only just returned to the cottage when Margaret arrived back with the children. Megan thanked her and said she really appreciated the rest and time on her own.

CHAPTER TWENTY

Over the last couple of nights as she lay in bed Megan pondered over Coleen's invitation. Trying to push all thoughts of it from her mind but she kept thinking of how exciting it sounded. She was just drifting off to sleep. Suddenly Evan and herself were woken by a loud bang in the distance. Evan pulled his trousers over his long underwear and Megan put a shawl over her nightdress. They checked the children who were both asleep.

When they went outside the neighbours were also outside wondering what the noise was. Evan and the rest of the men said they would go and see if they could find out what had happened.

Apparently, the Williams Brothers who were notorious in the area had decided to steal Coal from one of the trams. During their efforts they had somehow managed to dislodge one of the train couplings. This had worked itself loose and careered off the rails and down the hillside. The tram had stopped just inches from Mrs Davies's house at the end of Coal Yard Cottages. It was a miracle it had slowed down in time. If it had crashed into the cottages who knows what damage could have been done. Evan Megan and their neighbours certainly did not get much sleep that night as by the time everyone had discussed the disaster and gone back into their homes it was time for the men to go back to work.

The weekend arrived and Megan's mind was in turmoil. She wanted to go to the travellers get together even though she knew it was wrong. What made matters worse it was on the Sabbath and Megan had been brought up to respect that day. It was a time for going to church, families getting together and giving praise to the Lord. But the adventurous side of Megan longed to experience something different for once in her life. She convinced herself that if she went the Lord would forgive her this one error of judgement. She went to chapel as usual with Evan and the family then had Sunday dinner at Margret's. Then when it was time for the family to go to evening worship, she told Evan she was not feeling well. She felt so deceitful. Megan also knew tonight was going to be a long service as Pastor Phillips was preaching and he could go on for two hours. The families in the chapel always took the children into the vestry to keep them occupied. Evan kissed her on the cheek and told her to rest up.

Megan felt too guilty to make eye contact with him. As Evan closed the door behind him Megan gathered her thoughts. She knew she should not go but somehow, she had to. She once again checked the outside before she hurried across the fields. As she got closer, she could hear music playing and singing.

Then she did something terribly wicked she removed her bonnet and took the pins from her bun then let her hair fall loosely around her shoulders. She had on her Sunday dress but still felt drab and dowdy. As she tentatively walked towards the gathering Colleen came running to meet her and took her by the hand and up the steps into her caravan. She told Megan she had a present for her. Megan excitedly unwrapped the gift. It was a beautiful shawl, remarkably like Colleens but Megan's had beautiful emerald flowers on hers. Megan excitedly threw her beige knitted shawl onto the bed and replaced it with the one Colleen had given her. Colleen placed a gilt framed hand mirror into Megan's hand. Megan was shocked when she looked at herself in the beautiful mirror. The reflection that stared back at her was unrecognisable. She could easily have been mistaken for one of the travellers with her dark hair falling loosely onto her shoulders. Her complexion was flushed from rushing across the fields and to complete the effect the brightly coloured shawl around her shoulders. Colleen grabbed Megan's hand and led her towards the campfire. Two men were playing a catchy tune on violins accompanied by three girls hitting tambourines and dancing at the same time. Megan knew she must be conscious of the brief time she had here and not get carried away or distracted by her gay surroundings. Megan's heart beat wildly in her chest as she saw Paddy walking towards her. What an earth was the matter with her. She should only ever have eyes for Evan. It was as if somehow, she seemed to have lost her senses, it was as if a magical spell had been cast upon her. Paddy took Megan's hand and started dancing with her. Megan felt light headed and dizzy with the sound of the music ringing in her ears in the heady atmosphere. After twirling her around a couple of times the music slowed, and Paddy held her close. Megan looked into Paddy's eyes suddenly he leaned closer to her. His lips brushed her cheek, then the next thing she knew he was kissing her passionately on the lips. Megan found herself responding.

Then reality emerged what on earth was she doing. She was a happily married woman who loved her husband and family. Megan was overwhelmed with remorse for her deceitfulness and behaviour. She felt she had not only disobeyed Evan but also God for being so wicked on the Sabbath and afraid that God would punish her severely for what she had was doing. She pulled away from Paddy and apologised, why she did not know. Maybe it was because she had led him on. Paddy did not look in the least bit concerned he just stood there grinning at her. It was obviously only normal behaviour for him to dance and kiss the girls on such a night. Megan told Paddy and Coleen she had had a wonderful evening, but she had to rush back before the family came home from chapel.

She ran across the fields tears streaming down her cheeks. She could hear pastor Phillips's reprimand echoing in her ears "you wicked wicked girl".

As she approached the front door of the cottage, she could see people leaving the Chapel and making their way down Bedford Road. She opened the door quickly ran up the stairs removed the shawl from around her shoulders and hid it under the mattress. Suddenly realising she had left her shawl and bonnet in Colleen's caravan. Well one thing for sure she was certainly never going back there to retrieve it. Thankfully, she had another shawl and bonnet.

As she lay on the bed her heart was beating so fast in her chest, she had trouble catching her breath. As there was no sign of Evan or the children, she removed her dress and put her nightdress on. Her breathing now started to return to normal, she laid on the bed and pulled the cover over herself. Megan heard the front door open and Evan and the children entering. Megan felt dreadful when Evan slowly opened the door to the bedroom and peeked inside. Megan feigned sleep. It was sometime later after Evan had settled the children into bed that Evan crept in beside her. He kissed her gently on her cheek before he turned over and went to sleep. Megan buried her face in the pillow to stifle her sobbing.

The following morning before Evan left for work, he inquired if Megan was feeling better.

Megan lied and told him she had a good night sleep and was feeling much better. Then Evan kissed her and left for work.

It was raining heavily that day the dark miserable weather matched Megan's mood. Thankfully, the children were good so Megan black leaded the grate, a job which she detested doing, she thought it penance for her deceitful behaviour over the past few weeks and vowed to be a dutiful wife putting all thoughts of Coleen, Paddy, and the travellers out of her mind.

CHAPTER TWENTY ONE

Megan was concerned when Evan arrived home from the mine on Tuesday evening. He did not give her his usual happy smile or remove his cap and jacket his demeanour was worrying her. Then he told her he would have a chat with her later once the children were settled into bed. As Megan washed his back and shoulders Evan was tense, she did not want to pursue the matter.

Megan took the children and put them to bed. Typically, Bron seemed to take longer to settle down. As Megan rocked her, her thoughts started to wander. She became anxious, it was most usual for Evan to come home in this frame of mind, because even when he had experienced a difficult shift down the mine, once he walked through the door, he left it all behind him. She was afraid to go down, what if Evan had heard about her visiting the travellers camp when he had strictly told her directly never to set foot there again.

When she descended the stairs, Evan was sitting in the arm chair by the fireside. Megan removed the warm broth from the stove, buttered some bread and placed them upon the table.

Evan simply nodded and walked towards the

table. Megan could feel herself shaking as she walked towards the table. She bravely put her hand over his and asked him what was wrong, silently praying it was nothing to do with her escapade.

Evan clasped her hand and she felt relieved. He went on to explain that there had been a problem at Parc Slip today. Geraint who was the safety officer had spoken to the supervisor regarding his concern over one of the pit props, he was afraid it had been dislodged and appeared loose. Bob Matthews the supervisor dismissed the matter and told Geraint to get on with his work. When Geraint argued with him, Bob told him if he did not get back to work, he would dismiss him. One of the other men intervened and Bob got angry and told him if he did not mind his own business, he would dismiss him as well. Then Evan went on to explain by this point all the men were concerned. Bob then pushed Geraint and said this was his final warning. Geraint was about to punch Bob but one of the men held him back, as he knew if Geraint hit Bob, it would be instant dismissal and Geraint was a married man with six children to support. Bob then went red in the face and told Geraint he was sacked and if any of the others had something to say they would join him. Evan told Megan that the men were having a meeting in the White Lion tonight and if Geraint was not reinstated, they were all coming out on strike.

The following morning as Evan left for work, he kissed Megan on the cheek and said, "try not to worry Cariad". Megan smiled and hugged him closing the door behind him.

After Evan left Megan began to clear the table and took the pots and pans into the scullery. She then sat in the armchair by the fireside, she felt sick inside. Over the last couple of months Megan had been glad that Evan had left Brynddu Colliery to work in Parc Slip, as they were far better off money wise. She also knew when Bryn heard of the situation in Parc Slip, he would smugly tell Evan and Owen they had both been foolish to leave Brynddu. He had told them both that the supervisor there was a pig of a man who cared little for his workforce and only thought of himself. Whereas the supervisor at Brynddu had always been a fair and just man who looked after all the miners. Megan knew this would be the last thing that Evan and Owen needed to hear, she only hoped it would not cause animosity between the brothers.

Megan knew whatever the outcome of tonight's meeting she would not be able to dissuade Evan from coming out on strike, because all the men were loyal to each other even if it meant putting their jobs on the line. The thought of Evan being out of work terrified her. They would have no money coming in and if the strike was not resolved quickly, she did not know how they would survive. Megan also knew that when it came to management, they would take the Foreman's side and there were so many men looking for work in the area that it would not affect coal production. It all seems so futile, she could understand them backing Geraint, but he was one man and for so many other families to suffer hardship did not seem fair, but she knew the other mine workers would never see it that way.

She waited for Evan to come home but could tell by the look on his face the decision to strike had been made.

Neither herself or Evan slept well that night and it was with a heavy heart that Evan left for work the following day. It was going to be an exceedingly long day waiting for Evan to finish work that evening.

Megan went to the village to get some provisions everyone was discussing the dispute at Parc Slip. Then it was further unwelcome news when she called in to see her mother-in-law.

Margaret had fallen earlier that morning; she had been putting washing on the line and tripped. She had badly cut her knee and hurt her wrist. Doctor Thomas had called he said fortunately no bones had been broken. He had strapped her wrist up and told her to rest for a couple of days. Typically, Margaret was angry with herself. Megan told her she needed to take the doctor's advice and both her and Elizabeth would look after her for a change. Margaret simply nodded her head and muttered under her breath. Margaret told her it was not just her the girls needed to look after William's chest had been bad again and he had difficulty breathing. She said he was resting in bed now. Megan made a cup of tea for Margaret and took one up for William. Poor William looked dreadful, he seemed to be struggling for every breath. Megan propped his pillows up and held the cup for him to sip his tea. She told him he was not to worry Margaret was alright after her fall and they were both in capable hands with her and Elizabeth. The only thing about today was because Megan had been so busy, she had not had time to worry about the mine.

Elizabeth took over for Megan to go home as she knew she was anxious. Megan busied herself preparing food. Her stomach was doing somersaults as she saw Evan walking past the window. When Evan entered the house, he told her there was no need to worry there would be no strike. Megan was so relieved.

Evan went on to explain the events that had taken place that day. He said all the men waited outside the entrance to the mine for Bob Matthews to arrive.

He said they stood for an hour and there was still no sign of him. Then they could see Bob Matthews walking towards them accompanied by the tall erect figure of Daniel James the Manager. Two other figures walked behind them, the men recognised the one he was a representative from the Ogmore Coal and Iron Company. They later found out that the other gentleman was from the North Navigation Company that had taken over the running of the mine in 1889.

The men braced themselves they knew their dispute with Bob Matthews was out of their control.

Daniel James explained to the men the matter between Bob Matthews and Geraint Jones had now been resolved and the men were ordered to commence work immediately before any further production was lost.

Geraint Jones then made an appearance and walked towards the mine entrance. All the men proudly followed him.

Evan told Megan that during their shift they ask Geraint what had taken place to change Bob Matthews mind. Apparently, Geraint Jones's father-in-law owned the local butchers in the High Street in Cefn. He was well-respected and knew some influential people. Both Evan and Megan enjoyed a pleasant supper after all the turmoil. Evan took some food to his parents as he wanted to put his father's mind at ease. Both Megan and Evan slept soundly that night.

The following day as Megan and the children walked up the hill towards Margaret's house, Megan was concerned to see Pastor Phillips bike parked outside. She hoped William had not taken a turn for the worse during the night. Thankfully everything was fine. Pastor Phillips wife had baked a fruit cake for Margaret and William which he was kindly delivering.

Megan was relieved as she walked through

the door despite her fall Margaret seemed a lot brighter today. She was a little concerned as Pastor Phillips had gone upstairs to visit William and she was worried that he would stay too long and tire poor William out.

Elizabeth and the baby arrived not long after Megan. Whilst Margaret sat with the children Elizabeth and Megan cleaned and did some baking. Margaret thanked them both and said she was so lucky to have such attentive daughter in laws. Later that day Elizabeth and Margaret took the children for a nice long walk hoping the fresh air would tire them out.

Over the next two weeks Margaret's arm had healed, and she was back to her old self but looking a little frailer after her fall. Doctor Phillips had visited William and advised him to rest for another couple of weeks and when he was feeling stronger to get plenty of fresh air into his lungs.

When the men had heard the news, they knew their parents would not be able to manage without William's wage. So, Bryn, Evan and Owen had decided they would all give their parents money every week until William was fit to go back to work. William and Margaret were not happy with the arrangement they both knew if William went back to work it would be detrimental to his health, so they gratefully accepted their offer.

CHAPTER TWENTY TWO

Megan and the children were sitting around the table having breakfast when they were disturbed by someone knocking the door. Megan was surprised when she peered outside and Robbie, Mair's eldest child was standing there. He grabbed Megan's hand and pleaded with her to come quickly as his new baby brother or sister was coming. Megan grabbed the children and went next door. It was complete carnage in Mair's house. Mair was pacing the floor holding her stomach. The older children were running around and shouting, Mabel the youngest was screaming the place down. Both Dafydd and Bron were delighted to be in Mair's house and joined the rest of the unruly clan.

Megan told Mair she would run up the hill and quickly fetch the midwife. Fortunately, Enid Evans the midwife was at home, she told Megan to go and sit with Mair while she sorted out her bag and would follow her down.

When Megan returned to Mair's cottage Rachel had arrived from next door and was attending to Mair. Rachel had made Mair a cup of tea and was trying to control the unruly children.

Enid arrived accompanied by an extremely large

woman. Enid helped Mair upstairs to the bedroom in readiness for the impending birth.

Megan knew the large woman was Mair's mother. She placed her suitcase onto the table and proceeded to take charge of the children. She thanked Megan and Rachel for their assistance. Then put on her pinafore with one hand and started grabbing the children with her other hand. Megan was relieved to get back into the quietness of her own home.

Margaret was becoming increasingly concerned over William's health. He did not seem to be improving despite his complete bed rest. His breathing was laboured, and he was coughing up black sputum. Because William had been coughing so much during the last couple of nights Margaret had been unable to sleep and was feeling worn out. She was so glad she had two good daughters in laws to help her.

She also felt blessed that she had raised three such considerable sons, as without their help she knew her, and William would have struggled to survive. Margaret was anxiously waiting for Doctor Phillips to call. He went upstairs to check on William, he told Margaret just to be patient even though it was exhausting for William and distressing for Margaret. Dr Philips went on to explain that by coughing up the coal dust he was getting rid of the coaldust in his lungs. He told Margaret if there was no improvement in a week to send for him again.

Thankfully, there was no need after three days of severe coughing followed by exhaustion William started regaining his strength, the coughing had eased, and the colour was coming back into his cheeks.

The following week William felt well enough to come downstairs and sit in the backyard and enjoy the summer sun.

Six weeks have now passed, and William and Margaret were taking short walks, and a combination of fresh air and sunshine had aided William's recovery period. William told the boys he now felt well enough to go back to work. Unbeknown to Margaret and William the Roberts boys had all been fortunate to have extra shifts which had supplemented their income and enabled them to help without their own families suffering.

Megan was relieved that William was now on the mend. She had been concerned for the past couple of weeks as Evan was looking exhausted with all the extra shifts and was not his usual cheery self.

It was Dafydd's fourth birthday on the 1st of September which was only three weeks away. She had planned a special trip for him. They were all going to go to the nearby seaside town of Porthcawl. Dafydd was fascinated by trains. He loved to watch as they made their way to various locations carrying coal and iron ore. Megan's plan was to take him and Bron to Porthcawl on the train. A surprise she had not told him yet as she knew he would be so excited she would not be able to stop him talking.

It had been a difficult couple of months and a trip to the seaside would do them all the world of good.

Megan had baked a batch of Welsh cakes, and she was going to take some to Margaret and call next door and give some to Mair. She had been busy knitting the last two weeks and had now finished the matinee coat for Mair's latest offspring.

When Mair's mother called Megan inside Megan thought she was in the wrong cottage. The old grate had been black leaded and was positively gleaming. The children were playing quietly and Mair's mam was nursing 11-month-old Mabel who sat contentedly on her lap. Dafydd and Bron sat with the children and joined in their game.

Megan went upstairs to visit Mair who was sitting up in bed knitting. Even though the baby was only two weeks old Mair looked well. The baby was fast asleep in the crib next to the bed. Mair told Meg that her mam was staying for one more week, but Mair said she did not want her to leave. She said she had been wonderful taking over the cooking cleaning and caring for the children. Mair also told Megan since her mother had been there, Gwilym had not been drunk once. Mair laughed and told Megan it was because he was afraid of her mam. Megan could quite understand as the size of

WENDY JOHN

Mair's mam would put fear into most men.

CHAPTER TWENTY THREE

Elsie Dawson's husband carried the final piece of furniture into number 7 Mill Row. It was her grandmother's rocking chair, Elsie told Wilf to place it alongside the fireplace. She gratefully sat down, feeling quite worn out it had been a busy two days, but now the house had been cleaned and all the furniture put in place, she gave Wilf and her eldest son Michael a shilling to go and get themselves a well-deserved pint of beer in the White Lion public house which was situated not far from their new home. Her other son gave her a disgruntled look when she told him 15 was far too young to go into the pub. Gareth was angry as he said he had done his fair share of the moving and was not a child anymore. Especially as he was starting work underground in Parc Slip Colliery on Monday, Elsie nodded and agreed with him but said it was against the law.

She called the girls downstairs to play so Gareth could go upstairs to the bedroom out of everyone's way. The girls asked if they could go across the road and play in the nearby fields. Elsie told them not to go too far as they did not know the area and she did not want them getting lost. Both the girls ran off holding hands and smiling happily glad to be in their new environment.

Elsie sat contentedly and looked around her new home. The small living room looked out across beautiful green fields in the distance. There was a small scullery in the back where she would be able to do her own washing, and two bedrooms upstairs. She would go up later and put the dividing curtain in the larger of the two bedrooms to separate the boys and the girls. There was a shared privy in the yard behind, but the family were used to that.

It had been a big decision for Elsie and Wilf to move to Wales from Birmingham. There was no shortage of work there due to the industrial revolution, but due to the influx of people housing conditions were poor. Many large families lived in back-to-back houses.

Elsie and Wilf had occupied one of these houses from the day they were married. It had been hard enough when there was just the two of them but when the family came along it was very crowded. They only had one room which was their living room and kitchen and there was a cellar underneath. There was communal toilets and washrooms in the yard outside the properties. The family slept on mattresses downstairs in the cellar which was cold and damp.

Recently a lot of these properties were being demolished due to such poor living conditions.

Elsie and Wilf had hoped for one of the new terraced houses but after five long years of waiting nothing had materialised. Rebecca their youngest daughter who was five years old had developed pneumonia last winter she was so ill they thought they were going to lose her.

Wilf had heard about the collieries in South Wales, he knew the communities were smaller and housing conditions better.

Two months ago, Wilf and Michael had visited various areas in Wales checking out work and housing availability.

They became lucky when he saw the Manager of Parc Slip mine. He said they were looking for new men as the pit was expanding. He said he would be able to offer Wilf and both his sons regular work. He went on to tell him that one of the houses in Mill Row had recently become available. Wilf could not wait to return home and give Elsie the news. He had been to visit the house with the boys and knew Elsie would be delighted especially with Rebecca's deteriorating health.

Elsie found it hard leaving the friends she had made in Inge Street, but they were all delighted for her when she told them she was moving to a new house in Wales, and she would have a living room scullery and two bedrooms all to themselves. There were many tears shed they wished her well and told her with the new living conditions Rebecca would not have to suffer another winter with her bad chest.

Elsie felt quite melancholy as she sat there thinking of her close friends Maggie and Doreen. She knew she was going to miss them they had always been there for each other through many tough times but looking around her new surroundings she knew her, and Wilf had made the right decision. She had not said anything to Wilf, but she was terrified of him and her boys going underground in the dark coal mine, she prayed they had not made an unwise decision, putting accommodation before the boys well-being.

Her mood was broken by the girls running back into the cottage clutching bunches of primroses in their hands.

CHAPTER TWENTY FOUR

Megan sat on the wall by the well she could feel the heat of the warm summer sun beating down onto her back. The children were happily running around enjoying themselves in the field behind. Everything felt so calm and peaceful. It had been a difficult couple of months. Feeling in a pensive mood Megan looked towards the hills. Because there had been so much happening with Margaret and William there had been plenty to occupy her thoughts which fortunately left no time for daydreaming. Once again, she had that restless feeling, she had made a promise to herself that she would not venture back to the Waun to see if the travellers were still there, but now she began to wonder. She felt she must go back one more time just to say goodbye before they moved on. Her chain of thoughts was interrupted by Dafydd and Bron running back. Dafydd was overly excited he said he had made some new friends, but intimated they talked funny. Megan asked Dafydd to explain what he meant. He reiterated they are very friendly, but they talk funny. Megan looked across and two young girls were clutching bunches of flowers and walking towards Mill Row.

Then Megan realised what Dafydd meant she had heard a new family had moved into the Howells old cottage and they were from the Midlands.

William had now returned to work and Evan no longer had to do the extra shifts. Megan was relieved it was nice to have her old Evan back what with the extra work, no fresh air just the dust from the mines and the worry of his parents it had all taken its toll on Evan, and he had been exhausted the last few weeks.

Megan spent a restless night she knew it was wrong but there was a longing inside her just to see Paddy and Colleen one more time.

She called to see Elizabeth the following morning and asked her if she would mind the children as there were a few jobs she needed to do. She felt guilty when Elizabeth smiled warmly and told her she would be happy to look after them. Megan felt apprehensive as she slowly walked towards the Waun, guiltily looking around her she wandered on her way. She approached the clearing, stood, and listened. There was no sound, complete silence, in that instant she knew the travellers had moved on. Megan walked into the clearing and took in the scene. There were several burnt patches where campfires had been. Large holes in the ground left by the dogs digging. Indentations left from the caravans.

A great sadness came over her and tears fell down her cheeks. Despite what everyone had said about the travellers Megan had liked them and enjoyed being in their company, she thought back to June and how excited and alive she had felt. She was about to walk away when she noticed a strip of tarpaulin still attached to a tree making a small tent like covering. She peered inside, there was a small wooden box and on it was placed several handmade paper roses. Underneath was a parcel covered with leaves. Megan looked inside and found her shawl and bonnet that she had left behind on the night she run away from Paddy. As she picked up the shawl several bangles fell out, she knew these were the ones she had admired on Colleen's wrist. In that instance she knew if Colleen and Paddy had been able to write they would have left her a message. She felt touched by such a gesture and relieved in some small way that they had moved on because now there would be no temptation to come back and even though she felt sad Megan now knew she could get on with her life and the happy memories she had of Colleen and Paddy would remain in her heart forever.

When she got back home to her cottage, she placed the flowers and bangles in her bottom drawer and covered them with a blanket, her precious memories hidden from view. Megan enjoyed a cup of tea and a chat with Elizabeth when she picked the children up, she then contentedly walked back home.

CHAPTER TWENTY FIVE

Megan was keeping her fingers crossed that the warm sunshine would last until next Saturday. Evan had a well-deserved Saturday off, and they were eagerly looking forward to the seaside trip to Porthcawl.

Megan felt so many mixed emotions about the family's trip to Porthcawl, she could never bring herself to visit and always tried to push all thoughts of her home town out of her mind., but she knew the children would love a trip to the seaside and it was a special birthday treat for Dafydd.

The children were in bed and Megan and Evan were sitting on the wall opposite their cottage enjoying the last of the evening sunshine. Megan was concerned when she saw Bryn descend the hill and walk towards them. She felt nauseas and hoped William and Margaret were both alright.

Bryn said Elizabeth had asked him to call she asked would it be alright with them if Elizabeth himself and the baby went with them to Porthcawl on Saturday. Megan was disappointed she knew it was selfish, but she had hoped for a family trip. Evan looked towards Megan for an answer, but then Bryn went on to explain he thought the fresh air might do Elizabeth good as she had not been feeling well the last couple of weeks. Before Evan had chance to say anything Megan smiled and said yes, the more the merrier.

Megan had packed a small wicker basket that Rachel had lent them with provisions for their seaside trip. Dafydd was extremely excited on the morning of his 4th birthday, William had made him a small wooden train engine and a bucket and spade for Dafydd and Bron. Thankfully, the sun was shining. It was annoying as there was a train line from Tondu to Porthcawl that carried coal and iron ore, but the nearest passenger train went from Pyle station to Porthcawl which was about a mile away.

Both Elizabeth and Megan had the younger children safely positioned on their hips with their Welsh fashion shawls tied neatly around them securing the children. When Dafydd got tired both Evan and Bryn took it in turns to carry him on their shoulders. Dafydd was jumping up and down with excitement when he saw the old steam train chugging along the tracks.

As the train approached Porthcawl Station, Megan tried not to think about her childhood days here, too many memories flooded her mind, both good and bad. Fortunately, the children's excitement took over and Megan knew it had been the right decision for the children. Dafydd reluctantly got off the train and waved it goodbye,

Bron shouted and copied him.

The station at Porthcawl was filled with families all looking forward to their visit to the seaside. You could smell the fresh clean air as it filled your lungs. They all walked excitedly along the resplendent promenade. Evan and Bryn took an excited Dafydd and Bron to the beautiful beach. Where they contentedly filled their new buckets with the soft golden sand. Megan and Elizabeth sat inside the bandstand and rested, taking in the splendid Panorama.

Two magnificent hotels were positioned facing the promenade. The large Esplanade Hotel and the smaller Marine Hotel. They both sat watching as a couple of horse drawn carriages pulled up into the carriage way for some of the wealthy visitors to alight and enter their respective hotels.

Megan and Elizabeth sat chatting about how nice it would be to be rich and dress like the ladies entering the hotels. With their silk dresses, pretty bonnets, and parasols. They could have sat for hours taking in the scenery and listening to the brass band playing, but as it was nearing lunchtime, they knew the men and the children would be getting hungry, so they made their way along the lower promenade and onto the beach. The picnic was enjoyed by both the adults and children alike all feeling quite ravenous due to the sea air. In the distance they could see large throngs of people with children gathering, it heralded the arrival of the Punch and Judy Show. It had been an entertaining hour with much laughter enjoyed by all.

Sadly, all things must end and their day at the seaside was now coming to an end, and they needed to make their way back to the train station for their return journey home. Two tired tearful children had to be carried back from the beach. Dafydd and Bron had only been on the train for five minutes before they both fell fast asleep. Somehow the journey back up to Cefn from Pyle seemed endless as they were all tired after the seaside air. After putting two weary children to bed Megan laid beside Evan, it had been a wonderful day. She still wished she had been able to persuade Evan to look for work in Porthcawl when they were first married. Megan also thought it would have been so much healthier for them all being able to enjoy walks along the long promenade, instead of inhaling the constant cold dust that hung in the air around them.

CHAPTER TWENTY SIX

Megan and Elizabeth had taken the children for a walk and were making their way back to see Margaret who was now back to full strength after her recent fall. Margaret put the kettle on and buttered some Bara Brith for them to enjoy. Little William who had just started sitting up was happily gurgling besides Dafydd and Bron who were playing alongside him. A large cheeky grin appeared on Elizabeth's countenance as she went on to explain the reason, she had been feeling ill for the last two months. She said her and Bryn were quite dumbfounded it did not seem possible after waiting for 10 years for a baby and next spring God willing, she would have a new brother or sister for William.

Megan hugged her and Margaret gave her a small tap on her shoulder. Megan said she needed to get back to bake some bread, the children asked if they could stay with Margaret. So, Megan made her way back home. She was about to open her front door when she noticed Rachel beckoning her. Rachel grabbed her hand and pulled her inside her cottage. Megan refused tea as she said she had one at Margaret's, so Rachel poured her a refreshing glass of homemade lemonade which they took to the yard outside. Rachel's small courtyard was looking very pretty, it consisted of a variety of wooden pots planted with various flowers. Rachel said she wanted Megan to be the first to hear her news. Megan thought that Rachel was going to say she was expecting but that was not the case.

Megan and the family attended Siloam Chapel, but Rachel and Thomas visited various chapels depending on where Thomas was preaching. Rachel went on to explain her and Thomas had been called to a meeting at the Chapel last Sunday where the Reverend Pryce Davis from West Wales had asked them to attend along with the elders of Nebo Church. The Reverend Pryce Davis was a staunch believer in education and helped build and open new school rooms in West Wales and a few in this area. He said the small school room in Ffordd y Gythraith which was a tiny hamlet situated a short distance from Cefn were seeing an increase in the number of children attending. Rachel told Megan that both herself and Thomas had a good educational knowledge, and the Reverend asked them if they would be interested in running the school, with the added advantage of being able to rent a small, terraced house in the village.

Megan knew the village of Ffordd y Gyfraith and its close-knit community, she was quite envious of Rachel. No wonder she was so happy not just for herself but the fact that Thomas would no longer have to endure the hardship of working in the coal mine. Megan hugged Rachel and said she would miss her but she was only a short distance away so they would be able to keep in touch. Although Megan felt happy for Rachel and Thomas, she also felt a sadness inside. She felt things were changing in Mill Row what with the new family moving into Number 5, and once Rachel and Thomas left there would be new people at Number One. Megan had not met the new family yet but just hoped they were friendly. The main thing that concerned Megan was when people left you were never sure who your new neighbours were going to be.

CHAPTER TWENTY SEVEN

Dawn was just breaking casting a shadow of light on Number 7 Mill Row. Elsie watched as Wilf and the boys made their way across the fields to Parc Slip Mine. She stood and watched until the figures became small silhouettes in the distance, she felt an uneasiness inside her body and a cold shiver ran through it. She pulled her shawl tightly over her shoulders and across her chest. It was with a heavy heart she walked towards her grandmother's rocking chair sat down and put her head in her hands and wept. It had been two months since they had moved to Wales. She loved the warmth, cosiness, and extra space of her new home but she felt as if she had sacrificed one child's life for another. Rebecca was blossoming she no longer coughed and had started putting on weight and there was a healthy glow on her cheeks. It had been the right decision to move here for Rebecca's health. Sadly, her heart was now breaking for her youngest son. Wilf and Michael had both settled into the life of a miner enduring the darkness and long shifts down the mine, but this was not the case with Gareth. He had been afraid since his first shift down the mine. He was quiet and withdrawn when he got home. He had started having nightmares and crying out in his sleep. Elsie sat and tried to comfort him he told her he was afraid of the darkness in the mine and terrified that the lamps would go out. He said he was afraid the mine shaft would collapse, and he would be buried inside unable to get out. Wilf and Michael had tried to ensure him that even though it was dark they were quite safe there and nothing was going to happen. His young sons fear had affected Wilf and he blamed himself. He felt he had been too hasty in moving from Birmingham but like Elsie he could see the change in Rebecca's health. Wilf had looked for other employment in the nearby brickworks and surrounding farms for Gareth but was unsuccessful. He asked Gareth if he could just be patient and brave to wait it out in the mine and as soon as he found somewhere else for him to work, he would be able to leave. Gareth knew he had to overcome his fears for the family's sake.

Elsie had only recently become acquainted with some of the neighbours. Mair who lived in Number 2 and Megan and her family in Number 3. As she had not known them long, she did not want to burden them with her concerns. She knew she must get involved more in the community, so she had decided the family would be attending Siloam Chapel this Sunday. Wilf and the boys were not too keen on this idea, but Elsie told them it would be a good opportunity to meet other people from the village.

CHAPTER TWENTY EIGHT

Owen was becoming increasingly restless he first noticed it last Saturday night whilst enjoying a couple of beers with Bryn and Evan. They were both content with their families and life down the mine. Owen now felt ready to settle down and have a family himself but unfortunately Abigail's father when he had given his permission for him to court his daughter, he insisted they wait until next year to get married.

When Owen first set eyes on Abigail he thought she was something way out of his league. He had enjoyed the excitement of chasing her and finally capturing her. He used to enjoy the excitement of their clandestine meetings. It had been a year now and as much as he enjoyed Abigail's company, he no longer felt he loved her, he now began to think it had just been infatuation.

He also felt that Abigail had changed since she had become friendly with Rachel the new school teacher. Abigail had tried to persuade Owen to join their church groups which she now attended every Tuesday evening. Abigail got quite upset when Owen told her he was quite happy attending church with his family but had no wish to join Rachel's group. Owen wondered if Abigail had told her father she was attending these meetings as her family were members of St Theodore's church in Kenfig Hill which what is an Anglican church.

This was another matter that concerned Owen, he had been brought up in the Welsh Baptist Church and Abigail's background was Anglican. He knew her father had hoped he would attend church with Abigail and to please him he had attended once but felt it was not for him.

Once a month on a Sunday he had been invited to join the Parry family for Sunday lunch, he had found this a tiresome affair. Abigail's father liked to play the Lord of the Manor and was full of his own importance. Abigail's mother was a strange creature. Small in stature and thin with unusual, pointed features when he looked at her, she reminded him of a small bird. She did not possess a good deal of conversation and if she did speak it was usually followed by a nervous little laugh. Abigail's beauty certainly did not come from her mother.

On these occasions Abigail's brother Timothy his wife and two young children attended. Timothy's wife was a joy to be with. She was attractive vivacious and the life soul of the party. Timothy however was like his father and thought he was a cut above everyone else. They had two young daughters unfortunately they took after Timothy and were quite a haughty pair.

It was during these visits that Owen noticed the class difference. The only pleasure he got from these gatherings was when young Lizzie the maid brought the food into the large dining room. Her face would light up when she saw him, and she gave him the most endearing smile.

It was Abigail's birthday next month and for a special treat Owen was taking her to the new tea rooms which had recently opened on the promenade in Porthcawl. He was not looking forward to this he would much rather go to the White Lion with his brothers or even one of the churches social events. Owen had decided he would give it another month and if he felt the same, he would break the news to Abigail, he knew she would be upset but also had the feeling that she was not happy in their relationship anymore.

It was not just Abigail that was making Owen feel restless. He was fed up with his life as a miner, he thought by going to Parc Slip from Brynddu things might have improved, but even though the pay and the conditions were better one mine was much the same as another.

The last two months had been particularly difficult for him Wilf and his two sons had started working there. Owen had a particular fondness for young Gareth. The poor boy had been terrified from his first day working underground. Owen had taken Gareth under his wing and tried to reassure him. Owen took him along different sections of the mine and introduced him to the other boys of his age. Mining was hard enough for older men but extremely difficult for the younger boys.

Over the last couple of months Owen had made another decision in his life. He had decided after his father had been so ill, he did not want to end up coughing up black dust in twenty years' time. His friend Daniel Evans and his brother John had been telling Owen they were thinking of going to Pennsylvania in America. They had heard there was plenty of work there due to the expansion of railroads, petroleum, iron and steel production and manufacturing.

Owen had a tidy nest egg put by as he had been saving for his marriage next year. He knew this would enable him to travel and sought out lodgings whilst he looked for work there. The more he thought about this the more he wanted to do it. He had discussed America with Bryn and Evan. The idea had not appealed to Bryn, but he could see he had given Evan something to think about. The only obstacle standing in his way was his parents and he knew once he had made up his mind it was going to be difficult to break the news to them.

CHAPTER TWENTY NINE

Megan and Evan sat opposite each other by the fireside. Megan was sewing and Evan was reading. Every couple of minutes Evan glanced towards Megan then put his head back down. After much debating with himself he addressed Megan. Evan told her Owen had decided to end his romance with Abigail. Megan was not surprised to hear this, in fact, she had been expecting it. When she had seen Owen and Abigail together over the past few months, she could see things had cooled in their relationship.

Evan said Owen was going to tell Abigail next month which was November. As he did not want to upset her over the Christmas period. Megan looked at Evan and could tell there were further matters he wanted to discuss. She was a little concerned at the anxious expression on his face and hoped there were not problems at Parc Slip and that all was alright with his parents. Megan was quite taken aback when Evan told her that Owen was thinking about emigrating to America in the New Year.

Evan then went on to explain all the new opportunities that were on offer in America.

Megan was fortunate to have such a considerate husband as Evan she knew a lot of the men never discussed matters with their wives. If they wanted to do something even if it was moving to the other side of the world, they would have expected their wives to agree without any discussion or disagreement and just go. Megan quite liked the idea. She told Evan to think long and hard about it, as she knew Margaret and William would be heartbroken when Owen gave them the news, but it would be a double blow if Evan Megan and the family went as well.

Evan walked towards Megan took her face in his hands and kissed her passionately telling her he loved her very much and was a lucky man.

Evans' mood was pensive over the next couple of weeks. Megan knew that Evan had been hoping for Megan to tell him she did not want to go to America and as far as he was concerned that had would have been the end of the matter, now Evan was torn. It was a wonderful opportunity, but Evan had always been far closer to his parents then Owen or Bryn. He decided he was not going to rush into anything. He wanted them all to have a nice family Christmas then see how he felt in the New Year.

Megan and Mair had received an invite to a small social gathering Rachel was holding. She asked them to invite some of the other neighbours in Mill Row. Their new neighbour Elsie was delighted as it would give her the opportunity to meet new people. Tommy pig's wife Alice said she would love to go with them. They tried to persuade Lilly, but she declined the offer.

It was a rare occasion when the women had the chance to all dress up and go out together leaving the children with their respective husbands. Even though it was a bitterly cold December night at least it was not raining. It was too dark to take a shortcut across the fields, so they walked together through the lanes to the small hamlet of Ffordd-y-Gythraith.

All the women were envious when Rachel greeted them at her front door. Her house was larger than the cottages at Mill Row. Rachel had placed the large wooden table alongside the wall in her living room. A brightly coloured tablecloth was placed upon it, and it was laden with dainty provisions for the ladies get together.

Rachel introduced them to two of her new neighbours and all the women greeted one another and started chatting away. Megan had been there about ten minutes when there was a knock on the door and Abigail was shown in. Megan felt uncomfortable seeing Abigail after Owen had ended their relationship, fortunately, there was no cause for concern. Abigail walked towards her hugged her and gave her a kiss on the cheek. Megan felt relieved to have the chance to speak to Abigail. Abigail told Megan she missed Owen but did not bear him a grudge. She said she had kept herself busy helping her mother looking after some of the poor families in the community. Rachel kept them all entertained by singing and playing the piano. All the ladies sang various Christmas carols enjoying a glass of Rachel's delicious homemade elderflower cordial. The evening had lifted all the ladies' spirits usually the only time they had a get together was when there were social gatherings in Chapel but during these get togethers they were usually accompanied by their husbands and children. It had been a most enjoyable evening and very thoughtful of Rachel. It had been lovely spending time with her and seeing her new home.

CHAPTER THIRTY

The next couple of weeks had been busy with the usual cleaning baking and making presents for Christmas.

Megan was feeling so much better now her morning sickness was over and both her and Evan were looking forward to the arrival of the new baby in June. They had not said anything to the rest of the family yet in case Megan miscarried again. They were both praying everything would be alright.

Elizabeth insisted on doing Christmas dinner for all the family. Even though there had been quite a battle going on as due to Elizabeth's condition Margaret and Megan had wanted to do it. They could see how much Elizabeth wanted to do it, so they reluctantly agreed. Once again Elizabeth was blooming in her pregnancy and the change in Bryn was unbelievable.

Christmas 1891 was a special Christmas. Whether it was because apart from Margaret and William the families knew Owen had made his decision and would be leaving to make a new life in Pennsylvania in America at the end of January. Also, after many discussions and with a new baby due Evan and Megan had made the decision to remain in Wales. They thought they would announce their news after Owen had told his parents of his plans. They thought it would give Margaret and William something to look forward to, not just having one more grandchild next year but two.

It was a strange New Year's Eve for Bryn Evan and Owen, they celebrated at the White Lion as they had done ever since they had been old enough to drink.

Only this year was different Bryn and Evan were celebrating having new additions to their families but there was a feeling of great sadness with Owen going to America.

Once again whilst enjoying a pint of beer together Owen tried to persuade his brothers to go with him. Bryn said even though the work was hard he enjoyed working down the mine his Foreman and Managers were fair men, and he enjoyed the camaraderie of his fellow miners. He said now he had become a father after ten long years this was all he had ever wanted.

Evan could see Owen needed some reassurance he was doing the right thing. He did not want to hold him back with his future. Evan told him he had discussed America with Megan and they had both decided with a new baby due in June they needed to stay here for this year. Then to offer Owen some comfort and encouragement Evan told him if Owen settled into his new home in

Pennsylvania and the work prospects and housing were good himself and Megan would join him the following year. This lightened Owen's mood and give him a great deal of comfort. It was a good night at the White Lion, and everyone was in high spirits.

Suddenly the door burst open, and Alice stood there. All the men turned around as you never saw a woman in the bar in the White Lion. Alice was terribly upset. she said Tommy had fallen whilst feeding the pigs and could not get up. If it had been anyone else only one or two men would have volunteered to help whilst the others continued sipping their pints. As this was Alice it was different outcome altogether men were clambering towards the door to help. The Roberts brothers and a few others said they would help her they quickly finished off their pints and followed Alice home.

Poor Tommy was a sight, and it was hard for the men not to laugh. Apparently, the ground was quite frosty, and Tommy had slipped on a patch of ice. Poor man had lost his balance and the bucket of pigs swill he had been holding had tipped all over him. He was covered in carrots, potato peelings and various other vegetation. He tried not to be embarrassed as the men helped him to his feet. Alice was brushing him down to remove the debris. They managed to get him through to the scullery and into the high-backed chair in the living room. One of the men went to the pub and brought him a Brandy to help with the shock.

Alice thanked them all and asked if they would like anything to drink. The men declined the offer thanked her and said to let them know if there was anything further, she needed as they would be in the White Lion for another hour. As soon as the men were far enough away from Alice's cottage, they all looked at each other and released the suppressed laughter they had all been holding back. The event of Tommy's fall had certainly been a memorable event to the New Year's Eve celebrations and taken Bryn and Evans mind off their brother's impending departure.

CHAPTER THIRTY ONE

Margaret as usual showed extraordinarily little emotion when Owen gave them his news. She simply hugged him and said we will miss you son. William who was of a more sensitive nature hugged his son with tears in his eyes. William told him he was making the right decision. He told him spending long hours down the coal mine finished many a man off before they reached 40 years of age.

All the family and several friends had been invited to attend a large get together to ensure Owen had a good send off. Several kegs of beer had been brought to the house it was a bittersweet night. Abigail had also arrived to let Owen know there was no bad feelings between them, she hugged and kissed him and wished him a happy and prosperous future. There was lots of laughter and many tears. Owen would be sorely missed but all the family knew he had thought long and hard about his decision and this was what Owen wanted. Owen left for pastures new the end of January leaving a large gap in all the Roberts family's lives. Margaret and William were delighted when Evan and Megan told her she would be having another grandchild in June to keep her busy, this lifted her spirits.

December and January had been bitterly cold months and the start of February was mostly rain. Elizabeth had not been well she was experiencing a lot of back pain. Megan thought this not surprising she was huge. Megan had made her a new dress and pinafore as she had outgrown her last dress. Elizabeth laughed as she told Megan she might need another dress if she kept growing as she had another two months to go. It was a cold dark February evening when there was a knock on Megan's front door. Margaret was standing there with an anxious look on her face. She said Elizabeth's waters had broken and she had gone into labour. Megan told Margaret to go and sit with Elizabeth and she would run up the hill to fetch the midwife.

Megan's heart was beating fast in her chest with fear as she ran up the hill. This baby was coming too early, and Megan was worried about Elizabeth who had been so excited to be expecting a brother or sister for William. She prayed all would be well. She waited as the midwife prepared everything and they walked back down the hill together with Enid explaining to Megan sometimes babies came early especially twins. Margaret was upstairs attending to Elizabeth. It was strange Elizabeth was one of very few women who had straight forward labour. As she gave her final push a small dark head appeared. The baby was small, but this was expected at seven months. Margaret took charge of the baby whilst Megan and the midwife continued to care for Elizabeth. Elizabeth was experiencing further labour pains. Then to everyone's surprise except the midwife baby number two arrived. This one was also small but healthy. The midwife checked Elizabeth and the twins over and informed Margaret and Megan that both mother and babies were healthy. No wonder Elizabeth had been so big. Daisy Elizabeth had weighed in at 4 pound 2 ounces and Daniel Bryn was 4 pound 6 ounces. This was one of the few times that Megan had seen Margaret show any emotion. She knew tonight had brought back all the sad memories of the twin girls she had lost all those years ago. Megan told Margaret to go home, and rest and she would sit with Elizabeth and the babies tonight. She felt a warm glow as she looked at Bryn holding the babies and Elizabeth laying on the pillow with a tired but contented smile on her face.

The next two months flew by. The good thing about the Roberts Twins early arrival was it had taken all the families mind off Owen's departure.

Margaret and Megan were busy caring for Elizabeth and looking after the babies and young William. Instead of the usual Monday wash day everyday was now taken over with a constant stream of babies washing. Thankfully, the weather was good, and it dried quickly. Elizabeth and Bryn decided they would like to have the babies baptised during the Easter Service.

It was a beautiful warm sunny April Sunday. All the children in the Chapel took part in the Easter celebrations. It was lovely to hear their sweet voices singing special choruses. After the service and the baptism, a celebration tea was enjoyed by all the parishioners in the church Hall on Cefn Road. Megan felt content walking down Bedford Road on her way home. She loved her sister-in-law Elizabeth and seeing her proud face in Chapel which was filled with joy now she had the family she had waited so long for. William and his twin brother and sister were flourishing Dafydd and Bron walked ahead of Evan and Megan holding hands and skipping and singing at the top of their voices Evan looked at Megan with a beaming smile and proudly tapped her growing bump.

CHAPTER THIRTY TWO

Elsie and her family had now settled into their new life in Wales. Elsie's spirit had been lifted thanks to Rachel's intervention. Rachel had called to see Elsie and Mair to let them know some places had become available in her school room at Ffordd-y-Gyfraith and over the past couple of months Mair and Elsie had got to know each other whilst walking the children to school. Elsie had found it strange at first not having any children at home. Mair could not believe her luck with her three eldest children in school she now only had the two babies to look after. During this time Elsie and Mair had become firm friends. They had found they both shared a love to gossip.

Elsie would spend most mornings in Mair's cottage after they had taken the children to school. Elsie would join Mair at the large oak table and they spent their time drinking endless cups of tea and savouring the delights of Mair's Welsh cakes fresh from the griddle. Elsie now realised this is what she had missed most from Birmingham it was spending time with her old friends Betty and Doreen drinking tea and gossiping. Mair filled her in with the lives of all her neighbours in Mill Row and if Elsie had any gossip from the village or chapel, she would relate it to Mair. The latest piece of news they had to discuss was Teg Evans the Postmaster who had been carrying on with the Enid the midwife from Bedford Road. According to Mair this had been going on for over a year and nobody knew. Then apparently on a warm summers evening somebody had seen them together in the nearby woods. They both relished this piece of gossip. Mair told Elsie if Teg's wife found out she would swing for them both. She was a tiny woman but known for her fiery temper. It was reported that many a time she could be heard shouting and screaming abuse at Teg if he had not done things correctly in the small post office in Cefn Road.

Elsie loved her pristine environment, the neighbours, and the Welsh community in general. Everything would have been perfect if Wilf and the boys had other employment not being down the mines. The only good news was that Gareth was now more content his nightmares had ceased, and he had made friends with a few of the other boys employed at Parc Slip. Also, thanks to Owen Roberts he felt he had a future to look forward to and would not have to spend his life in the deep dark recess of the mine. Owen had promised him he would keep in touch sending him regular letters of his new life in Pennsylvania. Gareth had been visiting Rachel Thomas the school mistress in the evenings after his shift down the mine. She had been teaching him to read and write and he was a willing pupil. Gareth hoped by the time he received his first communication from Owen he would be able to read it.

Even though Gareth had learned quickly he did not want to show Rachel. Mainly because she had been a light in his dark existence. Instead of being fed up with the evenings after he had bathed and eaten, he would eagerly run across the fields to Rachel's house. He had decided he was going to be an awfully slow learner to enable him to have the pleasure of sitting alongside Rachel for as long as possible. He was quite besotted with her. He loved her smile and her voice, and she was beautiful to look at her husband was an incredibly lucky man. Whenever he felt afraid of the lights going out underground, he closed his eyes and pictured Rachel.

CHAPTER THIRTY THREE

The months of April and May just flew by. The days had been filled with glorious sunshine. The weather was a welcome relief as it had been a long hard winter with bitterly cold winds. Megan found it strange not seeing so much of Mair, but it was nice to see her happy with her eldest children in school and enjoying the company of Elsie who seemed to be settling well into the Welsh way of life. William was also looking better after his last bout of illness. Margaret was thriving now she had so many grandchildren to help look after. They had also received their first letter from Owen which was full of news regarding his new life in America.

He told all the family he missed them. He said he certainly did not miss being underground and it felt wonderful to breathe fresh unpolluted air. Owen told everyone he had managed to obtain work on the railroad. He said the work was hard and he was outdoors all weathers, but the pay was good and the hours he worked were not as long as his shifts down the mines. He had found lodgings with a lovely lady who was looking after him well. He told Bryn and Evan he missed their Friday nights at the White Lion, and it would take him some time to adjust to his new way of life.

He promised his mother once he was settled, he would look for the nearest Baptist Church. He told Megan he had several lady friends whose company he found entertaining but had not found the future Mrs Roberts yet.

The sunshine seemed to disappear when June arrived. It rained most days for the first two weeks. Megan had been experiencing severe back pain for the last two days and she knew it would not be long before the baby made its entrance into the world. Unlike Elizabeth's births Megan's had not been straight forward. The baby had been breach and the midwife had difficulty delivering it. In the end they had to send for Doctor Phillips at one point Evan had thought he was going to lose both Megan and the baby but thank the Lord they both pulled through.

Little Anwen was a tiny frail baby and the first six weeks had been a difficult and worrying time for them all. Once again Margaret had come to the rescue and tirelessly looked after both Megan and the baby. Elizabeth had also played her part despite being busy with her young family she had taken care of Dafydd and Bron.

It was the beginning of August before Megan was up and about and able to care for her family once again. She took things slowly going for walks in the fresh air with Elizabeth and Margaret. The families were all looking forward to next Friday the 26th of August which was the day of the annual St Mary's Fair. The last couple of years had been disappointing as it had rained heavily. Everyone in the village was praying this year they would have fine weather.

The Saint Mary's fair was a grand event enjoyed by families and children alike. People visited it throughout the borough. People brought their livestock to trade. Horses being one of the main trades. Many farmers were lucky enough to get a good deal on a new pony or cart horse. Gypsies would come with their caravans and park on the Moors at nearby Troes.

There was a large amount of beer tents frowned upon by the Temperance Society and Quakers. Unfortunately, as was usual at the Fair many of the miners and other workers saw this as an opportunity to let their hair down for the day and drank far too much of the strong ale. By the end of the day a few fights broke out and the local constable had to intervene.

There was a long avenue of stalls selling fruit and vegetables. Another spectacle was some of the side shows which had travelled from everywhere to entertain people. One year Megan could remember a woman performing with snakes and even a crocodile. There was 10 pin bowling and other games of skill and chance. When William and the Roberts family visited the Fair, the women would wander off and take the children to enjoy the small merry-go-round.

Whilst the men headed to the tent that contained the boxing ring where you could earn yourself some money if you fought against one of the professional boxers. Bryn had entered this contest two years ago but unfortunately, he had taken a bit of a beating. All four men had been given a sharp telling off when they returned to the women.

Megan was not looking forward to it with her usual zeal as Evan had been unable to get a shift off and had to work. She also knew William and Bryn would be missing Owen's presence this year.

Megan was awake most of Thursday night as Anwen would not settle. She would not take her ten o'clock feed and it felt strange as Anwen had always been such a good baby. She had tried rocking her gently but to no avail. Megan had also given her boiled water. Poor little mite looked worn out by three in the morning. Megan placed Anwen on her lap face down and gently rubbed her back. She finally took a feed at 4:00 o'clock. Megan was dropping off to sleep whilst feeding her as she was so tired. She quietly crept downstairs and placed her in the crib. Megan fell into bed alongside Evan who was snoring heavily, this usually kept her awake but not tonight. She placed her head on the pillow and fell into a deep exhausted sleep.

Evan had heard Anwen screaming during the night and knew Megan was exhausted. He crept quietly out of bed at 5:30 and kissed a slumbering Megan gently on the cheek. He was so disappointed that he could not attend the Saint Mary's Hill Fair and consoled himself with the thought that he had been fortunate to have had the previous two years off. He thought it typical the one year he was unable to attend promised to be a dry day.

Megan was surprised when she woke up to find Evan had left for work. She was a light sleeper and usually heard him but because of Anwen's restless night she had slept soundly. It was 7:00 o'clock and sunlight was reflecting through the small window panes. An exhausted Anwen was fast asleep in her crib.

Megan's peace was suddenly shattered by the appearance of Dafydd and Bron charging into the bedroom and jumping on the bed. Megan made her way wearily down the stairs. It was ridiculously hot in the living room, so she opened the door to let fresh air in, placing a heavy box in front of it to stop Bron escaping. Megan felt so tired she really did not want to go to the fair today especially as Evan had to endure his long dark dreary shift down the mine instead of spending time in the fresh air with his family. Megan knew if she did not go, she would be letting Elizabeth down as she was really looking forward to it. Megan and the children were eating breakfast at the table, their peaceful breakfast was disturbed by noises emanating from outside. She could hear shouting and strange noises. She moved the box and her and the children went outside to look.

Tommy had been trying to load his large boar onto the cart to take it to the fair, but it had it had escaped and was running down past Mill Row towards the fields.

Tommy was red in the face running after it closely followed by his three children. Alice stood outside her house with her hands on her hips and an annoyed expression on her face. Megan always found it an enigma how Alice who was quite refined had married Tommy they did not have anything in common but were incredibly happy together.

Everyone clapped and cheered as Tommy finally caught up with the boar and was leading it back up the road with a rope attached around its neck. You could not help liking Tommy he was such a character; he simply smiled and donned his cap to everyone given a small bow as he walked past.

Elsie and Mair were deep in conversation as usual. Even though it was only 7:30 in the morning thanks to Tommy's entertainment most of Mill Row were outside. The main topic of conversation was the day's outing to Saint Mary's Hill Fair. Elsie was glad she had Mair for company as Wilf and the boys had gone to work at Parc Slip.

Megan returned inside the cottage to prepare the day's picnic. Her spirits had lifted a little thanks to Tommy's boar.

CHAPTER THIRTY FOUR

At around 8.30am on the morning of the 26th of August 1892 Elizabeth Davies was just clearing away her breakfast dishes in readiness to leave for St. Mary's Hill Fair.

Suddenly it felt as if the very walls of Bay Cottage in Cwm Ffos shock. Her heart was racing when she realised that the explosion had come from Parc Slip Colliery. Her husband ran across the fields towards the colliery.

Meanwhile back in the village the shunting train brought the devastating news up the line to the brickyard sidings.

All the families were outside Mill Row having heard the explosion. Suddenly a woman ran past hair streaming out behind her shouting and screaming repeatedly that the Parc was on fire. She ran past the families outside Mill Row and continued running up Bedford Road towards Cefn Ridge. Everyone stood outside traumatised at the news, families who only an hour earlier had been looking forward to the day's events. Alice thanked God that Tommy had managed to change his shift today. The other residents in Mill Row felt relieved that their husbands and sons were employed at the

Brynddu Mine not Parc Slip.

Three women stood together their hearts racing in fear and trepidation. Kind friends and neighbours had taken care of their children. Megan, Mair and Elsie walked together through the fields to Parc Slip. Many other villagers were heading towards the mine from various locations all with one aim in mind.

In Aberkenfig, Kenfig Hill and Cefn people wept and waited for news of their loved ones. Megan, Mair and Elsie stood together with countless other families watching waiting and praying that their loved ones would be brought out alive. Men had come from all directions to volunteer and help to retrieve men and boys from inside Parc Slip.

The first few men who had been nearest to the entrance to the mine came out choking from the gas but alive. Further down the drift to North Fawr was entirely blocked by a fall after the explosion. Undeterred the rescuers worked towards the main slant. As night fell the bodies of the first victims were brought out. The rescuers worked tirelessly throughout the night. Sadly, now all hope was diminishing for men to be found alive. Then there was a glimmer of hope ventilation had improved and about 18 men made their way out. Then a further 25 men made it out though they were in a far worse shape. By Saturday evening all the workings had been painstakingly explored and the future of the rest of the men inside the mine looked grim.

As Megan, Mair and Elsie stood vigil outside the mine every time someone had come out, they hoped it would be one of their families. When the last lot of men were rescued one of them was carrying a young boy in his arms. Elsie pushed past everyone it was her Gareth barely recognisable through the coaldust, which had covered his body, but her heart wrenched when his sapphire blue eyes gazed into hers. He was weak but alive. The man placed his limp body on the ground besides Elsie she stroked his head as her teardrops fell onto his face. She sat beside her son hoping Wilf and Michael might still be alive.

As time went by the three women knew all was lost and they were not going to see their husbands again. Large groups of women were now dispersing and were making their way back home. The bodies that were found were taken up the hill and laid out in various chapels in the village. Sadly, not all the 112 men and boys were able to be identified due to decomposition and burning. With heavy hearts the three women united in their grief made the journey home, each departing into their own small empty cottages.

Megan looked around the empty cottage it still had the picnic placed on the table. She sat on the chair put her head into her hands and wept. Her body shook and her heart felt as if it was going to break in two. Margaret and Elizabeth arrived, and all three women held each other and wept together. This was a sad day for not only the

Roberts family but also for so many others.

Elsie warmed the water and filled the bath for Gareth. He just sat there as she gently rubbed the coaldust embedded into his back. Gareth sat there motionless just staring and not uttering a word. Elsie was silent as well united in their loss. Rachel had told Elsie she would look after the girls for a couple of days to enable Elsie to grieve and care for Gareth. Elsie helped Gareth put on his nightshirt and led him upstairs to bed. She placed the blanket over him as he was shivering due to the shock. She knew Doctor Phillips would call as soon as he was able to. As Elsie sat beside Gareth holding his hand the shock of the deaths of Wilfred and Michael hit her. Oh, how she wished she had never moved here. It was her worst nightmare something she had dreaded happening since her husband and boys went down the mine. It was no compensation to know there had never been a disaster at Parc Slip like this one. Her lovely cottage with all the extra amenities was now futile. She would give anything to be back in Birmingham in her dark damp back-to-back house. Just the thought of all her family still being alive and sleeping in those cramped conditions brought a flood of tears. She looked at Gareth who had now thankfully fallen asleep. Exhausted with shock and grief she fell asleep beside him.

Rachel had asked Mair if she wanted her to care for her children as well, but Mair had declined the offer. She needed her children with her now more than ever. For the first time in her life, she was grateful for her large unruly brood. Glad to have to be home away from Rachel's strict rules they ran around shouting, screaming, and fighting. Mair did not know how she was going to survive without Gwilym. She knew his reputation in the village when he came home in the nights from the White Lion after consuming too much alcohol, singing at the top of his voice, and disturbing the neighbours. The bitter arguments that would then ensue when they would both argue and shout at each other. Yes, he had been argumentative due to the drink, but he had never raised a hand to her unlike some husbands. Gwilym was completely the opposite character when sober a kind, caring and hardworking miner and a wonderful father. Mair was finding it so hard to curb her emotions but now she needed to be strong for the children. She dreaded having to explain to the older ones that they would never see their father again.

A dark heavy cloud of sadness shrouded Cefn and the surrounding villages. It had been an endless stream of mourning and constant Church and Chapel services throughout the vicinity. There was weeping at the grave sides as husbands' sons and brothers were buried. The sounds of the horse's hooves as they gently pulled the carriages to the final resting place could be heard along the quiet country lanes and along Cefn Road. There was no colour anymore as so many women wore their widow's weeds. The blackness of their garments echoed the emptiness they now felt inside. Life would never be the same again after such a tragedy.

It was late September and there was still warmth in the evening sun. The children were sleeping peacefully Megan opened the front door of her cottage and walked outside. She looked across the fields towards Par Slip. As she looked upwards a sprinkling of coaldust seemed to be drifting across. It fell upon the trees and the hedgerows. It appeared to sparkle as the sunlight filtered upon it. Tiny beads like black diamonds glistened. She felt Evans' presence even though she could not see him she felt it in her heart. The teardrops drifted slowly down her cheeks. She cried, not only for Evan but for all the other miners who had lost their lives on that fateful day in August 1892.

A SPRINKLING OF COALDUST

ABOUT THE AUTHOR

Wendy John

Wendy John was born in the seaside town of Porthcawl, South Wales. Wendy has always loved history and writing. She attended her local comprehensive school and her history teacher was inspirational. Since retiring from her job in the Local Authority she has spent her time reading and researching her surrounding area. This insight motivated her to write A Sprinkling of Coaldust.

Milton Keynes UK
Ingram Content Group UK Ltd.
UKHW041303181123
432831UK00004B/192

9 798391 782155